LOST IN SPACE ™

THE NEW JOURNEYS

Journey to the Planet of the Blawps

NANCY KRULIK

SCHOLASTIC INC.

New York Toronto London Auckland Sydney

No part of this publication may be reproduced in whole or in part, or stored in a retrieval system, or transmitted in any form or by any means, electronic, mechanical, photocopying, recording, or otherwise, without written permission of the publisher. For information regarding permission, write to Scholastic Inc., Attention: Permissions Department, 555 Broadway, New York, NY 10012.

ISBN 0-590-18941-7

12 11 10 9 8 7 6 5 4 3 2 1   8 9/9 0 1 2 3/0

Printed in the U.S.A.

First Scholastic printing, November 1998

For Amanda, who knows girls can do anything!

1
The Equation

"If y is 700, then x must be negative 452."

Will Robinson loudly announced the answer to his latest algebra problem. His fourteen-year-old sister, Penny, looked down at her watch and checked the time. Then she sat back, ran her fingers through her dark, spiky hair, and groaned. It had taken her little brother less than one minute to solve the complicated equation. And that wasn't even his best time.

Penny put down her laser writing utensil (better known as an LWU) and looked at her computer screen. She hadn't even come close to completing the problem, but it didn't matter. Even though he was four years younger than Penny, Will always beat her to the answer — and he always got it right.

When the Robinsons were back on Earth, everyone was always bragging about Will's brilliant mind. And when it came to math and science, Will was indeed a genius. He had created a nonworking model for a time machine for his fifth grade science fair — something not even adult scientists had been able to do. And more importantly, the Robinsons had proof that if given the proper energy source, Will's model would work. Unfortunately, Will's time machine would have to remain a family secret, since the Robinsons were stuck flying around in space, with no way to get home.

The Robinsons had planned on being the first family to settle Alpha Prime, a planet that would provide the human race with unlimited water, oxygen, and food. But their mission had been sabotaged by members of the evil Global Sedition — and by a traitorous physician known as Dr. Smith. Dr. Smith had been hired by the Sedition to kill the Robinsons before they could reach Alpha Prime. But Dr. Smith's evil plans had gone wrong in many ways: Not only had the Robinsons survived, but Dr. Smith was now stuck on board the *Jupiter 2* with them.

Unfortunately, Dr. Smith *had* managed to sabotage the mission — the *Jupiter 2* had flown way off course during the battle to harm the Robinsons. The spaceship was nowhere near Alpha Prime now. Or if it was, no one on board could tell. The Robinsons had no idea where they were. In short, they were lost in space. And as far as Penny was concerned, it was no picnic being lost in space with a little genius on board.

"You want me to show you a shortcut to the answer, Pen?" Will offered, interrupting his sister's thoughts.

What a showoff! "I can get it, Will," Penny replied sharply. "I'm just not into hurrying the way you are. I like to take my time." And that was the truth. Penny was good at math and science. Very good, in fact. Just not as good as her brother. But there weren't many people who were as good at math and science as Will.

"In an emergency, there's no time to take," Will countered. "If you can't do these problems quickly, you won't be able to calculate changes in your computer program in time to move your ship onto a different course."

"That's *Major West's* job, Will," Penny answered him. She

glanced over at the *Jupiter 2*'s pilot. He was busy checking the course of the spaceship. Penny sighed as she watched Don West run his hands absentmindedly through his thick dark hair. Penny had a secret crush on the handsome major. And *secret* was how her crush was going to have to remain. Major West only had eyes for Penny's older sister, Judy, the ship's doctor. And Judy's blue eyes were focused only on Major West.

"Well, maybe someday you'll be in charge of your own ship," Will suggested. "And then you'll need to . . ."

"What ship?" Penny argued. "In order to have my own ship I'd have to get back to someplace where there were humans, which means getting back to our own galaxy. And as you can see from the stars out there, little bro, we're nowhere near our own galaxy."

Will looked out at the unfamiliar constellations and sighed. Penny had him there. Penny smiled triumphantly. She had finally defeated her freckle-faced foe!

Maureen Robinson, Penny and Will's mother, shook her head at her two offspring. Mrs. Robinson's official capacity on board the *Jupiter 2* was finding and processing life sciences data and information. But she was doing double duty as the chief tutor for her two younger children.

"Okay, you two, I think we've had enough algebra for one day. How about we turn to literature? Have you both read the second act of *Romeo and Juliet*?"

Penny sat up tall and grinned. Literature! Now this was where she would really shine. Penny had always done well in her English classes. Communication was her strong point.

"I think the characterization of Juliet as too young to know . . ." Penny began to speak passionately about one of her favorite plays. She had so much in common with the main character. Like Penny, Juliet was fourteen years old. And Juliet also felt that the adults around her didn't understand what it was like to be a teenager.

"Mom, why do we have to study a four-hundred-year-old play?" Will interrupted. "What does it have to do with our lives?"

"It has *everything* to do with our lives," Penny countered. "People today still feel the same emotions. They still have the same prejudices. They still . . ."

"Uh, Maureen, could I have your attention over here for a second?" Penny and Will's father, Professor John Robinson, interrupted this latest heated discussion. "We seem to be having conflicting readings on the oxygen and temperature levels."

Mrs. Robinson nodded. "Okay, you two, you're dismissed," she told Will and Penny. "But I will be downloading three equations onto your computers for homework tonight — and I want you to reread all of Act Two."

Penny and Will stood up and prepared to leave the bridge. "Hey, Pen, I'd be glad to help you with those equations," Will said. "I . . ."

Penny didn't hear the rest of Will's comments. She had already popped her small, shell-shaped musical implant into her left ear. Now she couldn't hear anything except the heavy computer-generated bass beat of her favorite song.

Once Penny was back in her cabin, she reached under her bed for a special food pack she kept hidden there — dehydrated chocolate was better than no chocolate. Snacking between meals was expressly forbidden by her father — they had to hold on to their limited food supply for as long as possible — but this was an emergency. Penny needed comfort food. It was so hard having such a turbo brain for a little brother.

"*Blawp! Blawp!*"

A chimplike creature about the size of a large teddy bear leaped onto Penny's lap and stuck out its long tongue. Penny stroked the creature's shiny yellow scales and gave it a small piece of the chocolate.

"Hey, Blawp." Penny smiled as she looked into the animal's round blue cat's eyes. "How do you always know when I have chocolate around?"

As Penny took a bite of the chocolate pack, she lay back on her bed and gently stroked Blawp's skin. Blawp was just about the only good thing about being stuck on board the *Jupiter 2*. Back on Earth, her parents wouldn't even let her have a dog. But here she was in charge of caring for this awesome alien creature.

Judy had found Blawp while on an exploration expedition aboard a probe ship called the *Proteus*, which the Robinsons had discovered shortly after they had become lost. Judy had brought the little critter back on board with her and allowed Penny to keep her — on the condition that Penny be responsible for her. Penny had named the animal Blawp, for the sound she made.

Nobody could figure out what species Blawp was, or where her home planet was. All Judy could tell was that she was a member of some sort of self-replicating species who could change color based on their surroundings — sort of like a high-tech chameleon.

As Penny munched on her chocolate, she noticed the message light on her computer screen begin to blink. She used her remote control to call up the message. *Ugh!* It was those three math equations her mother had told her about. Penny looked at the screen and sighed. The problems were really hard. She could solve them on her own, but it would take her forever. She wished she could find a shortcut to the answer. But she would rather die than ask her little brother for assistance.

Just then Penny heard a soft whirring sound outside her door. *Robot!* Penny sighed with relief. Robot was the answer. Will had programmed part of his brain right into Robot's controls. Robot was twenty percent human. And he knew even more about math than Will did. He could help her with her algebra.

Penny opened the door. "Robot, could you come here?" Penny asked.

"I am programmed to enter any room on this ship," Robot replied.

Penny frowned. Robot seemed so human at times that she forgot that his mechanical brain took things so literally.

"I meant *would* you come here," Penny said.

The metal man immediately turned and rolled his way into Penny's cabin.

Penny pointed to the math problem on her computer screen. She opened the cap on her LWU and sat down at the screen. "Can you show me the simplest and quickest way to solve this? I don't mean give me the answer; just show me an alternate process that will eliminate several steps. I need to know how I can solve these problems quickly."

The lights in Robot's round glass head flashed on and off. And then, in his slow, halting voice, Robot began to explain the steps needed to best solve the first equation. Penny followed along easily and smiled when she got the end result. It felt good to be able to do the problem successfully.

As Penny followed Robot's instructions, she wiped a bead of perspiration from her brow. It was getting hotter and hotter in her room. She made a mental note to talk to her mother about bringing down the temperature levels on the ship.

"*Blawp! Blawp! Bloooop!*" Blawp began making strange throaty sounds. She raced quickly toward the cooling vent and jumped high to catch what few cool breezes she could.

"Poor Blawp," Penny said. The heat had obviously gotten to the creature as well.

Suddenly the lights in Penny's room went out. The computer screen went blank. Penny could hear her father's deep voice blaring through the ship's intercom system.

"Attention! This is an emergency. All unnecessary power systems have been turned off. I repeat, this is an emergency! Please put on your temperature control flight suits and report to the bridge at once! This is a Code Red command!"

2
The Heat Is On

Penny groped around in the dark until she found the shiny metallic flight suit. Sweat was pouring from her now — the heat was almost unbearable. Quickly, she slipped into her suit and flicked on the battery-operated light monitor in the helmet. She breathed a sigh of relief at the ability to see again. She turned on the temperature regulation switch. Instantly cool air began circulating around her body. Penny picked up Blawp and wrapped her in a temperature control blanket.

"Stay here!" she ordered Blawp. "If you stay completely still, that blanket should keep you cool enough." Penny crossed her fingers and said a little prayer as she walked out into the hall. She hoped Blawp would be all right on her own.

"I didn't know they had a sauna on board the *Jupiter 2*," Judy joked as she bumped into Penny in the hallway. Judy was trying to sound upbeat, but Penny could tell that her older sister was nervous. It was something in her eyes — which, other than a few wisps of her straight blonde hair, were the only part of Judy's face that Penny could see through her helmet.

"Hey, you two had better hurry up. Dad called this one a

Code Red," Will said as he ran past his sisters in the hall. "Must be pretty bad!"

Penny shook her head. *Nothing like stating the obvious.* Code Red was the top emergency code. Whatever was wrong, the family would have to work as a team to fix it. That was actually one thing Penny liked about being on board the *Jupiter 2* with her family. Back on Earth her father had hardly ever been around — he had been preparing for this mission almost twenty-four hours a day. That had left Penny's mom in charge of the family when she wasn't at work at the university as a life sciences professor. The family was hardly ever together. They never ate at the same time, played games together, or spent quiet evenings putting holographic jigsaws together like other families did.

But out here in space, the Robinson family was a real team. Penny's job was to take care of the video mechanics on the ship. Will was in charge of robotics. Only Dr. Smith had no job. He refused to help with anything, which was just fine, because the family found it hard to trust him to do any job correctly.

As Penny entered the bridge, she had to choke back a laugh. Her family, Major West, and Dr. Smith were all dressed in their shiny temperature control flight suits. That, combined with the way their voices were distorted through their speech vents, made everyone look and sound like a family of androids.

But one look at her father's tight body language made it clear that this was no laughing matter. His back seemed stiff against the chair, and his long legs seemed glued in place. His blue eyes looked grave and stressed. Something big was happening.

"Penny, please bring the left video monitor into focus," her father ordered.

9

Immediately Penny went over to the console and adjusted the focus on a large computer screen. Instantly a blinding yellow haze appeared on the screen. The viewer on Penny's helmet adjusted to the haze, placing a filter over Penny's eyes.

"That's a brand new star, folks," Major West told the others. "Literally just formed. It may be a baby, but it's got a lot of power. And we're stuck in its orbit."

"Can't we just hyperspeed our way through it like we did the last time?" Will suggested.

"I wish we could, son," Professor Robinson said. "But the ship's been damaged by debris breaking away from the star. We're leaking fuel. When we get out of this mess, we're going to have to plug the leak as it is. We can't afford to use what fuel we have on hyperdrive."

"Too bad we can't find a way to harness the energy from that star. Solar energy is one of the best energy sources around. In fact, if we'd started using it on Earth centuries ago, we might never have gotten into this mess!" Mrs. Robinson added.

Penny's eyes drifted over toward Major West. She could see her reflection in the shiny metal fabric of his space suit. She was shocked to see that she now looked as tense as her father.

"Never could refuse a mirror, could you, Pen?" Will whispered loudly as he caught her attention drifting.

"*Mirror!* Penny, you're a genius!" Major West shouted, jumping up out of his seat and giving her a comical sort of hug in spite of his bulky suit.

Penny looked stunned. "What did I do?" she asked, her heart thumping. Why couldn't he have touched her when she could actually feel it?

"You looked at your reflection. Don't you get it?"

Penny shook her head. Major West calmed down and explained his plan.

"Reflector shields. They'll force the star's rays to bounce back toward the star."

Penny nodded. "And that will cool the ship. Then we'll be able to harness the energy and use it to blast out of the star's gravitational pull, just like Mom said."

"See, you're a genius!" Major West said. "But this is gonna take a lot out of this ship. You guys had better all assume crash positions."

Major West moved toward the console and strapped himself into his chair. Professor Robinson took his position in the commander's chair. The others moved to their seats and tightly fastened their harnesses.

"This had better work, Major," Dr. Smith said. He folded one long leg over the other and crossed his thin arms across his chest. "We had better not crash into that sun. I'm certain that there is something in the war conventions against barbecuing a prisoner."

"You pig," Major West replied. "I'd love to barbecue you — with an apple in your mouth!"

"Name-calling is the language of the mindless fool," Dr. Smith snorted back. "Professor Robinson, I demand to know upon what scientific basis you are allowing this experiment to occur."

"Simple," Penny's dad replied. "I am allowing this to occur on the basis that no one else seems to have a better idea."

"We could ask Robot what the chances are of this working," Will suggested. "I'd just have to find him."

Penny gulped. She knew where Robot was. In her room. And if Will found out that the Robot had been helping her with her homework, he'd never let her live it down.

"No time for that, little brother," Penny said quickly. "I vote that we go for it."

11

"Will, Penny's right," Professor Robinson said. "It doesn't matter what our chances are. Without trying this, our chances are zero. The odds can't be worse that that.

"Shields up on the count of three, Major," he ordered. Major West nodded.

"One, two, three!" Professor Robinson said calmly. The crew of the *Jupiter 2* felt a slight bump as the reflector shields lifted into place.

"Temperature dropping," Maureen Robinson confirmed from her hand-held life sciences computer. "Eighty-two degrees and holding. Not exactly comfortable, but not life-threatening, either."

Penny and Will gave each other a thumbs-up. So far, so good.

"Okay, now for the hard part," Major West declared. "Prepare for solar power launch. Penny, care to do the honors?"

Penny nodded nervously. A solar liftoff was far more dangerous than a traditional one. For starters, the engines had to gather enough light to build to a high speed. And there was no real way to gauge that, the way you would with traditional fuel. There was no gas tank to check or radioactive canisters to count. You just had to approximate the amount of solar power available, and hope that it was enough.

Slowly she began counting down. "Ten, nine, eight, seven, six, five, four, three, two . . . one."

The *Jupiter 2* thrust forward with a force Penny had never felt before. It flew quickly for a few seconds, and then stopped dead. Penny could feel the ship reverse its direction. The *Jupiter 2* was being pulled back into the star's orbit!

"I hate to say I told you so . . ." Dr. Smith began.

"Then don't!" the others replied almost simultaneously.

"What's going on, Don?" Professor Robinson asked quietly.

"The ship's too heavy. We'll have to lighten it up. Hey, maybe we could throw Smith overboard," Major West joked. "Actually, we're going to have to remove at least one probe ship — maybe two."

"But those are for emergencies. They're like our lifeboats," Penny argued.

"There won't be any life to go on them if we don't release at least one," Will argued with his sister. He walked over to the console and said, "I'll start with the oldest one."

With a push of a button a small probe ship darted out from beneath the *Jupiter 2*. Penny watched as the tiny ship floated out into the dark sky. Almost immediately, the probe was caught up in the star's pull. With a flash of burning blue light, it exploded into a thousand pieces.

"Let's try it again," Major West said. "Hang on, folks."

Penny felt the ship jerk forward again. And this time it kept moving, faster and faster, away from the star.

"Yahoo!" Will cried out. "We are out of there. Way to go, Major West!"

Major West turned and took a mock bow. "Thank you."

Professor Robinson waited a few minutes before giving everyone permission to leave their seats. But once he did, everyone went about their duties. One by one, they lined up to be checked by Judy for dehydration and other harmful side effects of the extreme heat. As soon as he was given a clean bill of health, Will headed toward the robot bay to check on his charges. Penny ran a test of the video screens throughout the ship and discovered that two needed immediate repairs. She called down to the robot bay, requesting two repair robots on the bridge.

"They're on their way up, Pen," Will replied through his intercom.

Requesting the two robots made Penny remember that she had a robot to care for as well. Robot had been left in her room through all of this. Who knew what kind of state he was in?

Penny raced off the bridge and down the hall to her cabin. She was greeted by Blawp, who stood exactly where Penny had left her. She took the blanket off and gave the creature a big squeeze. "I'm glad you're okay!" Penny smiled as she pulled off her flight suit. Then she looked over toward her desk. Unfortunately, she could not say the same for Robot. He lay in a pile beside her chair. His head was tilted off-kilter, one of his kneecaps had come off, his left arm had separated from his body, and his front panel had popped open, revealing a maze of wires. Some of the wires were dangling loosely, having been shaken from their connections. The loose wires were twisted and knotted together. They would have to be completely sorted through, and Robot would have to be rewired before he could function in any way.

Penny gasped. How was she going to explain this one to Will?

3
The Joker

There was just one thing to do. Penny was going to have to fix Robot herself. She knelt down beside the broken metal man and looked at his wiring system. From up close, things didn't look too bad. Just a few loose wires. If Penny took her time and worked hard, she would probably be able to rewire Robot and send him on his way before Will ever missed him.

Penny picked up a red wire and a blue wire. Should she cross them, or place them straight? She tried to recall the robotics class she had taken last semester.

"*BLAWWWWP. BLOOOOOP!*" Blawp began to wail loudly. "*BLOOOOOP. BLAWWWWWP!*" The noise was deafening — louder than Penny had ever heard it before. And that included when the little creature sensed that someone nearby was eating chocolate ice cream.

"Will you cut it out?" Penny cried. "Can't you see I'm busy?"

But Blawp did not listen to Penny's commands. She continued her loud, mournful howls.

"Are you hungry?" Penny asked finally. She took a banana food pack from beneath her bed (another of her private snack stash) and placed it in a bowl. Blawp loved bananas. But this

15

time she didn't even sniff at the bowl. She just continued her yelping.

Penny didn't have time to figure out what was upsetting the alien right now. She had to fix Robot. She was able to reattach Robot's kneecap and arm with little difficulty. She straightened his head and laid him down flat. Now came the hard part. Quickly, Penny crossed two wires and reattached them. Then she reinserted one of the robot's electrode tubes and attached two green wires, one on either side of the tube. She used a laser screwdriver to tighten some of the screws and bolts in the robot's interior systems and quickly closed up his front panels. Finally, she helped the robot to his feet.

Almost instantly the lights in Robot's glass head began flashing on and off as he ran a systems check on himself.

"You took *some* fall," Penny said. "How are you feeling?"

"I am not programmed to feel," the Robot responded. "But my systems are all intact." The Robot's lights flashed on and off again. "Temperature control on the *Jupiter 2* seems stable but still quite high," he remarked.

"This is nothing," Penny exclaimed. "While you got injured the temperature was so high I thought we all would melt."

"We will have to refreeze the ice cream," Robot replied, obviously picking up on the word *melt*.

Penny laughed. When Will had programmed part of his brain capacity into Robot's mind, he'd programmed in some of his likes and dislikes, too. "Let me guess — you would like a strawberry ice cream pack right about now," Penny suggested.

Robot's lights flickered excitedly. "I will find Will Robinson. He would like some ice cream now as well, I am sure."

As Robot rolled out the door, Penny was very proud of herself. She'd successfully rewired Robot — with no help from anyone!

"*Bloop! Blawp! Bloop! BLAWWWWWWWWWWWP! BLAWWWWP!*"

Blawp was still crying out — and the volume was getting louder. Penny pulled out another food pack — melon this time — and tried to coax the creature to the food bowl. But nothing would calm her.

"What's going on in here?" Maureen Robinson knocked at Penny's door and opened it up. "Is Blawp okay?"

"Blawp *seems* fine. Maybe the heat got to her," Penny replied. "I'm trying to quiet her down."

Mrs. Robinson nodded, and pretended not to notice the food packs on Penny's floor. "Half an hour till dinner, sweetie," she said as she left the room.

Penny reached over and tried to calm her alien friend. She stroked gently at her scales, and watched as Blawp's skin color changed chameleonlike to the same shade of blue as Penny's sleeve. The stroking had a calming effect on the creature, and for a while she stopped squawking and began purring quietly, letting out occasional squeaky *blawps*. Penny laughed. Blawp sounded just like a big, scaly guinea pig!

In exactly half an hour, Penny went to the galley for dinner. She could hear Blawp crying out again as she walked down the hall. As sad as it made her to leave Blawp alone, Penny didn't turn back. Her father expected everyone to meet at dinner. No excuses. Penny figured he was making up for lost time. Besides, dinner was as good a time as any to analyze the day's events.

When Penny arrived in the galley, Will was already at the table, scarfing down his first helping of freeze-dried mashed potatoes and chicken.

Penny took her seat at the table and frowned as her mother placed a food pack on her plate. Penny was dying for a home-cooked meal. These space packs just didn't have that homemade touch.

"It's not too bad, Pen," Will said encouragingly as he bit into a piece of chicken. "You gonna eat your mashed potatoes?"

Penny shook her head and spooned the white mound onto Will's plate.

"Penny, you must do something about that infernal squawking going on in your cabin," Dr. Smith growled as he walked into the galley. "I was trying to take my afternoon nap today when that oversized lizardskin belt began singing like a tomcat on a fence. Now, I'm not one to complain, but . . ."

"Oh, no, you *never* complain," Major West said sarcastically. "Frankly, Smith, the only squawking I hear right now is coming from your mouth."

Robot wheeled himself over to Dr. Smith. He deposited a chicken dinner food pack onto his plate.

"What is he doing here?" Dr. Smith demanded of Will. "Isn't he supposed to be manning the controls or something?"

"Robot is welcome anywhere on this ship," Will insisted.

"It's you who are not welcome, Smith, " Major West added. "Besides, I have the ship on automatic pilot, and I can be contacted through the ship's computer system if there are any problems."

"Fine," Dr. Smith said with an obvious *harrumph*. "Can you also use the computers to quiet that Blawp?"

"Blawp has been a little loud, but I think all of the excitement just got to her," Penny admitted as she cut into the chicken on her plate. "She was bothered by the heat. Now that the temperature is back to normal, I'm sure she'll settle down."

"The animal appears to be calling out, perhaps to one of her own species," Robot remarked from the corner of the galley.

"I think the heat got to you, too, pal," Will said. "There are none of her species on board this ship."

"You are correct, Will Robinson," Robot answered. "And technically I can find no logical reason for the cries. But she *is clearly* attempting to communicate."

Dr. Smith frowned and stabbed his fork into his vegetables. He sniffed at the food and sighed. Dr. Smith continuously made it clear that the food packs did not satisfy his gourmet appetite. Finally he opened his mouth wide and ate a forkful of the freeze-dried veggies.

"AAAAHHHH!" he shouted. Peas and carrots flew from his mouth. "Chili . . . peppers," he blurted out. "Water . . . I need water!"

Penny and Will burst out laughing. It was hysterical to see the usually *very proper* Dr. Smith gulping down glasses of water as little pieces of potato ran down the side of his mouth and stuck to his goatee.

"Which of you little monsters put hot peppers in my food?" Dr. Smith asked, looking accusingly toward Will and Penny.

"Don't look at me," Penny said, choking back tears of laughter. "I wasn't anywhere near the food tonight."

"Me neither," Will said. "Robot took care of your meal, remember?"

"Obviously a robot did not do this," Dr. Smith barked. "Practical jokes are not part of an android's personality — unless you put them there, Will!"

"I haven't been able to program in human humor or emotional functions yet," Will snapped back. "But I'm working on it."

"Hey, what are you complaining about?" Major West teased Dr. Smith. "You're one lucky prisoner. You've got a flying roof over your head and three HOT meals a day!"

Dr. Smith looked so angry, Penny was almost sure she saw steam blowing out of his ears.

Maureen Robinson choked back her laughter and looked as stern as she could under the circumstances. "I don't know who is responsible for this, but it won't happen again, okay?" she said to Will and Penny.

Penny looked at Will with new respect. She didn't know her little brother was capable of pulling off such an awesome practical joke.

What she also didn't know was that Will was thinking the exact same thing about her.

4
The Cry of the Blawps

After dinner, Penny returned to her room. She was surprised to hear that Blawp was still howling for no apparent reason. And no matter which food pack Penny offered, the little creature refused to eat, preferring to use her mouth to shout. Finally, after much stroking and cajoling, she fell into a fitful sleep. She was probably exhausted from all that blawping.

Blawp had never made so much noise. Something was obviously wrong. Penny made a mental note to have Judy give Blawp a checkup — although it wasn't very likely that her sister would be able to detect something wrong with an unfamiliar species. Too bad they didn't have a space vet specializing in alien species on board.

Penny turned out the light and walked up to the bridge to check on the repairs Will's robots had made on the video monitors. She was surprised to see her father and Major West there. They were huddled over the ship's computer, running a few tests.

"We're going to have to fix that leak before long," Major West remarked. "We're losing too much power."

"We'll have to land the ship to do that," Penny's father responded. "It would be too dangerous to try a repair of that complexity during a space walk."

Penny looked out into the night sky. Land the *Jupiter 2*? Where? There were no planets visible for miles. But they'd better find one soon. From the sound of her father's voice, Penny could tell that the ship had suffered some pretty major damage.

Still, Professor Robinson remained calm and in control. "Penny," he called over, "can you call up a telescopic image of two hundred kilometers due north?"

"Sure, Dad," Penny replied, proud that her father viewed her as a valued member of the crew. She set the computer controls, pushed the red button, and waited. In less than a minute, a fuzzy image appeared on the screen. Penny could just about make out a few pieces of flying debris, but no planet came into view.

"Nothing," Professor Robinson said. "Try two hundred kilometers due south." Penny complied. But again, no planet came into view.

"How about one thousand kilometers," Professor Robinson suggested.

"No good, Professor," Major West interrupted. "This ship can't travel more than two hundred and fifty kilometers without repair. We're leaking fuel like crazy."

Penny tried to stop her hands from shaking. Without fuel the ship would be adrift, and it was sure to be pulled back into the gravitational force of that new star — or of any other star that might form. And 250 kilometers wasn't very much. Even if they slowed down to a crawl, they'd be motionless in an hour!

"Hmmm. How about one hundred and fifty kilometers due

west?" Major West suggested. "It's always been my favorite direction."

Penny took a deep breath. "Okay," she said. Once again she punched the direction and distance into the computer. The telescopic lens shifted to the west.

The screen was dark. Not even a star was visible. Suddenly a beam of bright white light appeared, like a spotlight in the dark sky. A star! Penny thought. Then a small marble-sized image of a light-blue and orange planet came onto the screen.

"I think I've found something!" Penny declared. "We're saved!"

"Not so fast, kiddo," Major West said. "We can't land there if it's a gas planet. We'll need to analyze the surface."

Penny nodded. Quickly she increased the telescopic power of the lens. It seemed to take forever for the image to come into a deeper focus. Finally, the planet appeared larger and clearer on the screen. Scanning the surface of the planet, Penny could just about make out a mountainous terrain. The surface of the planet was solid!

"Bingo!" Major West shouted out. "Professor, I believe I've found a repair stop."

Professor Robinson smiled. "Well, then, you know what to do. Go west, young man!"

Major West took his place at the console and began piloting the *Jupiter 2* toward the planet. Professor Robinson took the necessary steps to prepare the crew of the *Jupiter 2* for a landing.

"We are heading toward a planet for a repair stop," Professor Robinson broadcast through the ship's intercom system. "We will be arriving at our destination in approximately fifteen minutes. Prepare for landing."

Penny went to her cabin and made sure everything was secured. Blawp was still fast asleep, and Penny hoped that the impact of the ship landing on the planet would not wake her. She was not in the mood to be up all night listening to Blawp's howling.

But Penny had no such luck. From the moment the ship's landing gear went down, Blawp awoke from her fragile sleep. Instantly she began the wild screaming again.

"*Blooooop! Blawwwwwp! BLAWWWWP! BLOOOOP!*" Blawp cried.

Now Penny was getting really scared. Blawp's yells sounded nothing like they had before. They were loud, deep, and throaty, remarkably like crying. There was an odd pattern to Blawp's cries, too. The creature would wail for a few moments and then stop, as though waiting for a response.

"Penny, you will have to do something about that creature." Dr. Smith's voice boomed through the intercom in Penny's room.

Penny scowled at the intercom. Didn't Dr. Smith think she was trying? And who was he to complain? Blawp's noises weren't any more annoying than his constant whining.

Just then, Will knocked on Penny's door. "Is Blawp okay, Pen?" Will asked. "She's making some really weird sounds."

Penny shrugged. "I don't know what's wrong. All I know is no one on this ship is going to get any sleep tonight unless I figure out a way to help her. And whoever's going on that repair mission is going to need plenty of rest. I heard Dad say that fixing the leak is going to be pretty intricate work."

Will nodded. "I'm not sure how to get Blawp to stop making noise, but I think I have an idea on how to stop her from keeping us up all night. Bring her up to the holographic image room."

24

Penny didn't even ask Will what he had in mind. She just hoped that her little brother's idea would work. Penny picked up the alien and followed Will.

When they reached the holographic image room, Will placed a cartridge into the computer. Almost instantly the room filled with images of instruments. A holographic drum set, complete with cymbals, sat by the wall. A piano stood nearby, along with two guitars and one bass.

"What's all this?" Penny asked. "Are we going to play a lullaby or something?"

Will laughed. "I've heard you sing, Pen. We don't need any more weird noises on this ship," he teased. "But this image is soundproof — I've been practicing the drums here for a month now, and none of you have heard me."

Penny was amazed. Will had taken up the drums? That was pretty cool. First that practical joke he'd played on Dr. Smith, and now this. Will was full of surprises.

"Let Blawp stay in here tonight. Then maybe Judy can take a look at her in the morning," Will said.

Penny nodded in agreement. She hated leaving the little creature in this environment, but she had no choice.

As she and Will padded back toward their cabins, Penny looked back at the holographic image room. She could see that Blawp was still howling. She just couldn't imagine what she was trying to say.

5
The Planet

The repair crew was up bright and early the following morning. Penny could hear her parents talking in the hall as she awoke.

"We have no idea what we'll find on that planet, Maureen. With our surveying equipment malfunctioning, we don't even know if there are any life-forms there," Professor Robinson explained. "I don't think it's a good idea for both of us to leave the ship."

"Judy will be here to watch out for Will and Penny," Mrs. Robinson answered. "You'll need me to analyze the atmospheric conditions, and to help determine if there *are* any life-forms on the planet."

"You tell him, Mom!" Penny said as she came out of her room. "Stop worrying about us, Dad. I'm not a child anymore. I can help Judy take care of Will."

"All right, I can't fight all of you," Professor Robinson agreed. "Penny, you man the remote cameras from aboard the *Jupiter 2* while your mother and I join Major West on the surface."

"Cool," Penny responded. "Um, I mean, roger, sir."

"Do you want to take Robot with you, Dad?" Will asked as he walked down the long hallway. "I can get him ready in a few minutes, once I find him. He wasn't in my room when I woke up this morning."

Just then Dr. Smith came barreling down the hallway. "I've had quite enough, you two!" he shouted at Will and Penny. "Penny finally gets that alien monstrosity of hers quieted down and I start to get into bed, only to discover that someone has short-sheeted it — folded the top sheet in half so I couldn't get under the covers. And the more I tried to stick my feet in, the more I ripped the sheets." Dr. Smith angrily held up a bedsheet. Right in the center were two huge holes in the shape of Dr. Smith's bony legs. Obviously it had taken Dr. Smith a while to figure out that he wasn't going to be able to stretch out.

Picturing Dr. Smith forcing his big feet through the white sheet made Will laugh so hard, Penny thought he was going to lose it completely. Penny choked back her laughter so intently that she let out a loud snort through her nose.

"Will, I thought I warned you about practical jokes," Mrs. Robinson said slowly.

"I had nothing to do with this," Will argued. "Why are you blaming me?"

"Don't look at me," Penny added. "I was with Blawp and then I logged onto the computer to do my reading homework. You can check the computer log."

"Well, *someone* did this. And I do not appreciate it," Dr. Smith said. Then he turned angrily and stormed off, dragging the destroyed bedsheet behind him.

Maureen and John Robinson looked at Will and Penny and shook their heads. "Try to stay out of trouble while your dad and I are on the planet's surface, okay?" Mrs. Robinson said.

"Cool trick," Penny congratulated her brother once their parents were out of earshot.

"I swear it wasn't me," Will replied.

Penny smiled. "Sure, Will. Anything you say," she said as she went off to feed Blawp.

By the time Penny got to the bridge, her parents and Major West were suited up and ready to go.

"I have no idea where Robot has gotten to," Will said as he delivered a small square-headed robot to his father. "But this smaller A17 model should serve all your purposes. It's programmed to analyze liquid, mineral, and temperatures. Not as smart as Robot, but it will do."

"I'm sure it will be fine," Mrs. Robinson said. She bent down and kissed Penny and Will on the cheek before putting on her protective helmet. "We'll be back before lunch."

As her parents and Major West headed toward the exit hatch, Penny sat down at the video controls and focused in on the surface of the planet. She fought back tears as she brought the picture into focus. It was always hard watching anyone leave the protection of the *Jupiter 2*. This mission was especially dangerous because the ship's external communication devices had been damaged during the pullaway from the star. Will and Penny had no way of contacting their parents in case of an emergency.

And Penny knew there was a much larger problem. The Robinsons always did a preliminary scan of a planet before disembarking. The scan of this planet showed something strange, and potentially dangerous. On the opposite side of the planet, the video cameras showed a series of small igloolike structures made of a thick cementlike substance. Will had hypothesized that they had been created to keep out the intense heat. And although there were no signs of life on the planet, someone or something had built those igloos. Perhaps the creatures that built them had left the planet for a cooler place, or perhaps they had died trying. Then, of course, there was that scary possibility that they were still alive and nearby, waiting and watching the *Jupiter 2*.

Obviously Will was thinking the same thing. "Penny, you remember what Robot said last night, about Blawp trying to communicate?" Will asked his sister. "What if there's something out there — something dangerous? What if she was trying to warn us to stay away from the planet? What if Mom and Dad are in danger?"

Penny took a deep breath. "Mom said they'd be back before lunch," she said in a strong voice. "I believe her."

"I just hope they aren't *somebody's* lunch," Will murmured.

Penny flicked on the holographic video system and watched as the rescue team's holographic images were beamed aboard the bridge of the *Jupiter 2*.

"Looks like it's pretty hot out there," Will said as he checked the *Jupiter 2*'s external thermometer. "Even in those temperature-controlled suits, they're not going to be able to work out there for long. They're going to have to do the work in short shifts. And we'll probably have to take turns going out there."

"Looks like this planet is going to be home for a while then, huh?" Penny said. She pulled her dark hair back in a high ponytail. Even with the ship's air-cooling system, it was warm on board the *Jupiter 2*. Not unbearable, but slightly uncomfortable.

"How is Blawp this morning?" Judy asked as she entered the bridge. "I didn't hear a bloop from her all night."

"That's because she's in a soundproof holographic room,"

Penny explained. "But she's still wailing. And I can't keep her cooped up in there forever. Can you give her a checkup later, Judy?"

Judy nodded. "I'll go up and take a look — I don't know what I'm looking for exactly, but I'll try and compare some numbers. Just let me check the medical transmissions from the away team first."

The away team's space suits were specially equipped with devices that would constantly transmit their vital signs directly to the ship's computer.

"They're going to need a lot of cool liquids when they get back," Judy said. "That heat can cause dehydration pretty quickly." Then she left and went up to the holographic deck to check on Blawp.

Penny watched as Major West went beneath the front of the ship and began to repair the leak. Penny's mom was busy collecting samples of rock from the planet's surface. The planet looked dry and deserted, like an Earth desert during the day, when all of the animals were in caves or underground, escaping the heat. There seemed to have been some plant life at some point, because there were pieces of dried vines and leaves scattered on the ground. But there didn't seem to be any water. And that would make it hard for any life-form to survive there. Of course, Penny was thinking of Earth life-forms. Who knew what space creatures lived on? Even Blawp required hardly any liquid at all to survive.

"Hey, Pen, what's that?" Will asked her, pointing toward the center of a video image that appeared on an overhead screen. The image was of a small hill located a few yards behind the *Jupiter 2*.

"Looks like a lot of dry soil," Penny replied.

"No, there's something in that dirt. Some sort of pattern. Zoom in closer, okay?"

Penny shrugged. She didn't see anything, but it couldn't hurt to check it out. She pushed a blue button on the computer panel and the camera zoomed in for a closer look.

"Oh no!" Penny cried out. Strange alien footprints were clearly visible in the dirt, and they were headed directly for the ship.

6
Footprints

"Judy to bridge. Judy to bridge!" Penny cried out over the ship's intercom system. Judy came running to the bridge from sick bay. "What's wrong?" she asked. Penny pointed to the screen. The footprints were as large as an adult human female's.

"I knew it! I knew there was some sort of life on this planet," Will said.

"Robot was right. Blawp must have been warning us," Penny added.

Judy took control. "We've got to warn them," she said, calmly pointing toward the image of the away team. "Will, use the transmitter on the robot to contact Mom and Dad."

Will shook his head. "That robot is an A17 model. It doesn't have a transmitter. It's only designed to analyze materials."

Penny stared at the footprints. There was no way her parents could see them from their position. If only there were some way to get their attention.

Suddenly Penny's eyes lit up. She knew just what to do. She went over to the outer shield control buttons and slowly raised and lowered the rear reflective shield. The movement of the shield caused a flash of light to move through the sky.

"What was that?" Penny heard Professor Robinson's holographic image say. For a minute, Penny forgot that it was just his image and not her dad. Holographic images looked remarkably real, but they made skin look transparent, and they distorted voices. Watching them always reminded Penny of those antique 3-D movies she'd seen in the natural history museum. Of course, you didn't need to wear special glasses to see these, and the images were much more lifelike.

"It came from behind the ship," Major West's image replied.

Penny raised and lowered the shield again. She hoped one of the members of the team would rush over to explore, then warn the others before it was too late.

"We'd better see what's back there," Major West said. His holographic image left the bridge as his body moved out of the range of the camera.

"Bingo!" Penny shouted out excitedly.

"Great idea, Penny," Judy congratulated her.

Will didn't say a word. He just stared at Penny with new respect. Penny grinned back at him. "How's that for fast thinking, Will?" she asked.

"Nice going," he said admiringly.

Just then Major West's holographic image reappeared on the bridge. "We're not alone here, folks," the kids heard him tell their parents. "There's definitely another life-form here, and I have a feeling we'll be meeting them before too long."

"How's the repair going, Major?" Maureen Robinson's voice was calm, although Will and Penny could see her pulling at her sleeve, their mother's only sure sign of stress.

"I fixed the leak temporarily. But we can't safely leave this planet yet," Major West replied.

"Then we'd better learn all we can about the aliens on this planet," Professor Robinson said.

"Technically, honey, *we're* the aliens on this planet," Maureen Robinson reminded her husband. "I've gathered a lot of rock samples, which should help us determine what these creatures survive on. But it would help to get a cast of one of those footprints, and some soil. Maybe there's a trace of fur or skin in one of them." She turned and headed for the back of the ship to gather the materials they needed.

"I know Mom's right about gathering materials," Penny told Judy. "But I wish they would all just come on board now."

Judy patted her younger sister on the back. Then, suddenly, they heard a loud crashing noise from behind the ship. The three Robinson siblings waited for their mother's voice, but it didn't come.

"Maureen! Maureen!" Penny could hear her father's image call out anxiously. "Maureen," Penny's dad called again, a little louder. No response.

"Oh no! They've got her. Whatever's out there has got Mom!" Penny exclaimed.

"Not necessarily, Penny. Maybe she just didn't hear them or something," Will said. But his voice was unconvincing.

"There's no logical reason why she isn't transmitting anything to Dad and Major West."

Apparently, Penny's father believed the same thing, because at just that moment his image disappeared as he went behind the ship.

"Now they're both back there," Penny said, holding back sobs. "If anything happens to them, we'll be alone in the universe. Maybe Dad was right about both of them being out there together." Judy placed a gentle hand on Penny's shoulder. The three siblings sat there on the bridge and waited.

And then they heard the loud crunching of footsteps on top of dried leaves. Penny held her breath, wondering just what kind of creature was approaching.

"Wow, I'm sure glad to see you," Major West's image said aloud. "What happened?"

"I dropped some of my equipment," Mrs. Robinson replied. Penny felt a tear of relief run down her cheek. Her parents were okay.

"So why didn't you answer the calls?" Major West continued.

"I didn't want to draw any attention to myself, just in case there was anyone around. I didn't see anything, though."

Suddenly a bony, icy finger tapped Penny on the shoulder.

"AAAAAHHHHHH!" she cried out, jumping from her seat in fear.

"Penny, precious, you are a bit jumpy today," Dr. Smith snarled from behind her. "I merely wanted to know how long you were going to keep that blawping monstrosity of yours locked up in the holographic image room. I'd like a chance to visit someplace other than this overgrown sardine can for a while — even if it's only in a world of virtual reality."

"Let her out yourself, Doc," Penny replied angrily. "But beware — the only thing standing between us and a chorus of constant blawping is the soundproofing of the image room."

"Have your parents fixed the ship yet?" Dr. Smith asked, changing the subject.

"The leak is plugged, but we're probably going to be here a few more days," Will replied.

"Well, I hope your mother plans on increasing our cool air supply. I'm sure there's something in the prison code that prohibits keeping the temperature above eighty."

"Guess you took on more than you bargained for when you stowed away and tried to kill us all, huh, Smith?" Major West's deep voice boomed across the bridge as he and the Robinsons came on board.

"Don! You're back!" Judy raced over and gave him a squeeze.

"Mom! Dad!" Will ran to his parents. Penny smiled. Sometimes Will seemed so together and smart that it was hard to believe he was only ten. But then there were other times, like now, when his emotions took over.

"We were so worried," Penny said. "When Will spotted those footprints, we didn't know who or what . . ."

"Thank goodness you warned us about them, Will," Mrs. Robinson said.

Will shook his head. "That wasn't me. It was Penny. She had the idea to flash the reflective shields."

Penny smiled. "But it was Will who recognized the pattern in the sand as footprints," she added.

Will raised his hand for a high five. "Go team!" he shouted. Penny slapped his open hand.

Professor Robinson patted his middle child on the back. "Nice work, kids. We didn't spot anyone or anything, but there could have been something there — and there still may be. At least now we'll have time to analyze the data and try to figure out how long those prints have been there. Maybe we'll get some idea of what we're up against."

"*BLAWP! BLAWP! BLOOP! BLOOP!*"

Just then Robot wheeled himself onto the bridge. Blawp sat on his head, blawping and blooping wildly.

36

"Robot! Where have you been?" Will asked sternly.

"I am not able to compute exactly where we are at this moment," Robot said. "We are lost in space."

"Tell me something I don't know," Will mumbled angrily.

"When you sneeze, air rushes through your nostrils at about one hundred miles per hour," Robot replied.

"What?" Will asked. "What are you talking about? No one sneezed."

"I am simply telling you something you do not know," Robot replied.

"Did you let Blawp out, Robot?" Penny asked, anxious to change the subject.

"Of course. The creature is obviously trying to communicate. Someone had placed her in a soundproof room from which she could not do so. That seemed illogical."

"*BLAWP! BLAWP! BLAWP!*" Blawp leaped down from her perch on Robot's head and circled the bridge wildly, as if she were looking for something. Finally she settled down just below the air cooling vent.

"I could go with some cool air myself," Major West said. "It's hot out there. We're not going to be able to work for more than an hour at a stretch."

"Well, my preliminary data do have some good news," Maureen Robinson said. "The atmosphere is primarily oxygen. We won't need to carry any air tanks while we work, which should alleviate some excess carrying weight. That should buy us a few more minutes at each stretch."

"One thing's for sure. The combination of heat and stress is going to make us very thirsty and tired," Judy said. "I suggest we increase our number of hours of sleep. That will slow down our metabolism and allow us to limit our intake of drinking water. That supply could be in danger."

"And we'll have to cut down on showers — everyone gets only two minutes per day," Professor Robinson added.

Penny groaned. First her father had rationed food, now he was rationing water. There had been a time when Penny had felt like a space captive aboard the *Jupiter 2*. Lately she had begun to feel like part of a team on a great adventure. But once again, the *Jupiter 2* was beginning to feel like a huge metallic prison.

"Okay, now on to the most pressing point. There are definitely creatures on this planet. The question is, are they friend or foe?" Professor Robinson said.

"Here's what I know so far," Maureen began. "The creatures walk upright, although I suspect that they walk in a slightly hunched-over manner, because the footprints were deeper at the front of their feet." Maureen held up a plaster cast of the footprint.

Penny stared at the footprints. She'd seen that strange configuration of toes — two large ones and one small one in between, all with a ball-like structure on their ends — before. But where?

"We also know that the creatures on this planet communicate with one another, and they seem to travel in packs. Whether this communication is verbal or can be translated into written word, we can't be sure. I don't know much about the intelligence of the creatures, either."

"I think they must be pretty intelligent, Mom," Penny said. "They were able to construct those igloo things. Maybe they just didn't have the correct materials for keeping out the heat."

"They also breathe oxygen, don't they, Mom?" Will asked.

"Judging by the amount of oxygen in this atmosphere, I

would assume that they have evolved that way, yes," Mrs. Robinson answered.

"But don't they need water? Don't most oxygen-breathing creatures need water?" Penny asked.

Her mother nodded. "I think there is some water on the planet," she explained. "But very little. Still, judging from the amount of dried-out vegetation on the planet, I think there was more water until just recently. That's the puzzling part. My statistics show a dramatic shift in the atmosphere here. And my guess is it was very recent. It's probably related to the creation of that new star."

Penny listened to her mother, but her mind was on those footprints. Somehow she knew instinctively that the footprints were the clue that would put the whole puzzle together. But she couldn't say anything just yet. Will would be all over her, asking for proof. His scientific mind didn't leave any room for instinctive thinking. If she could just remember where she had seen those prints. . . .

"Well, I say we get this ship fixed as quickly as possible and get off the planet," Dr. Smith remarked. "Then it won't matter what these creatures are like."

Major West sighed. "Spoken like a true member of the repair team," he said. "Unfortunately, you are *not* a member of the repair team. I don't recall you volunteering to help us out."

Dr. Smith stared into the major's angry eyes. "Need I remind you that I am a prisoner on board this ship? "

"Thanks to you, we're *all* prisoners on this ship," Penny muttered, recalling the reason they were lost in the first place. "Besides, if what Mom says is correct, the creatures on this planet could be in great danger. And if that's true, it's up to us to help them."

"Penny, precious . . ." Dr. Smith began.

"Don't call me precious!" Penny complained.

"Penny," Dr. Smith continued, "I do wish you would stop this 'save-the-cosmos' act. Our main responsibility is to save ourselves."

"And no one knows more about that than you, right, Smith?" Major West barked, jumping to Penny's defense. Penny smiled at the major.

"Right now, I think we should eat a quick lunch and go to sleep," Judy said, jumping in to avoid another battle.

"Sleep?" Will's voice cracked with surprise. It was only lunchtime.

"If we want to find a way to best use our time, we need to learn to sleep in the daytime and do our work after dark. Desert animals hunt at night for that reason," she explained.

"Well, you all had better hope that the creatures on this planet don't hunt at night, too," Dr. Smith said eerily.

"*BLAWP, BLOOP, BLAWP!*" Blawp followed Penny to her cabin, screaming all the way. Obviously, the pressure of constantly crying and blawping hadn't done much to wear the little creature out. Penny held Blawp in her arms and stroked her skin. Instantly the shiny scales began to change color. Blawp felt warm, so Penny took out a juice pack and offered it to the creature. But Blawp would have nothing to do with the juice.

Penny felt helpless. And the constant noise was really starting to get to her. "What's wrong?" she asked quietly. Sometimes she was certain that Blawp could understand her. But if Blawp did understand her, she did not respond. She just kept honking and blooping and blawping.

"If you are going to keep crying like that, I'll have to put you back in the holographic chamber," Penny told Blawp.

"I'm afraid you won't be able to do that today," Professor Robinson said as he stopped outside Penny's door. "Creating one of those holographic images uses up a lot of power, power we can't afford to lose until we fix the ship completely. You'll just have to try and keep Blawp quiet."

"But how, Dad?"

Professor Robinson looked understandingly at Penny. "I don't know, but if anyone can do it, Penny, you can. You have a special rapport with that creature. And you are responsible for her. I'm sure you'll figure something out."

Penny listened to the screeching blawps as her father went down the hall. She knew it wasn't going to be easy. She also knew that her father wasn't just making a suggestion. It was more like an order.

Penny pulled out a food pack of bananas. Blawp walked over and sniffed at the food. Penny was pretty sure she even took a small nibble. Then, suddenly, Blawp started going wild. She tried to remove the wire mesh from the air vent in the cabin ceiling. And when she couldn't pull the cover free, she stood close to the wall and wailed into the vent.

Penny shook her head. It was going to be a long day. How was she going to sleep with all of this going on?

A few minutes later, Penny spotted Robot roaming the halls. "Hey, Robot, come here," she called out to him over the loud blawping sounds. "I want to ask you something."

Robot immediately wheeled himself into Penny's cabin.

"Yes, Penny Robinson?" Robot asked.

"Do you think something's odd about this planet?" she asked.

"Your mother has already revealed that the planet has undergone a dramatic change in recent times," Robot replied. "But other than that, I do not see anything odd about the planet. The terrain is actually quite similar to your deserts on Earth — although I do not believe it was always so. And I do not believe that the inhabitants of the planet are similar in form to humans."

Penny shook her head. She hadn't been asking for an analysis of the planet itself. "No. I mean, do you think this planet is making us change? Is something in its atmosphere causing a change in behavior? You know, Will suddenly becoming the jolly jokester, Blawp going mental?" Penny looked out through her window. "Do you think something out there is altering us? And will we ever be able to go back to the way things were?"

"I do not think that there is anything on this planet that is changing the behavior of the inhabitants of the *Jupiter 2*," Robot replied.

Penny breathed a sigh of relief. Robot was rarely wrong about things like this. "So you think this is all one big coincidence, then?" she asked Robot.

"My logic program does not allow for coincidences," Robot said. "There is a logical reason for everything."

"Well, what's going on?" Penny asked nervously.

Robot's lights blinked on and off. "I do not have enough data to come to a conclusive response," Robot told her. "But I will continue to search for information."

Penny took a deep breath as Robot wheeled away. She hoped he could come up with a conclusion before anything else bizarre occurred on the *Jupiter 2*. The next problem they encountered could be far more dangerous than some loud blawping or a few ripped bedsheets.

7
The Culprit Revealed

"*BLAWP! BLAWP! BLAWP! BLAWP!*"

By now Blawp's constant shrieking was becoming too much to bear. Penny had asked her family for any ideas or suggestions on how to quiet her down, but no one had any. And they were all extremely busy with their individual jobs. Blawp was Penny's responsibility. And it was a harder job than she had bargained for. At one point, Blawp actually ran out into the hall and charged up to the bridge of the *Jupiter 2*, howling all the way. Penny followed close behind, carrying food packs, juice containers, and cool towels. But none of her usual tricks seemed to work.

By the time night fell, Penny was exhausted. She'd had absolutely no sleep. And now she would be expected to go out and pull her shift on the repair crew. Suddenly Penny had new respect for her parents — could this have been what it was like when she and Will were babies? Ugh!

Judy was the first to come onto the bridge. "Rough day, Pen?" Judy asked.

Penny nodded. "Blawp hasn't shut up once," she said. "I don't know what the problem is. Did the noise keep you up?"

"Not too bad. It was hard to hear Blawp in my room once you guys were on the bridge."

Will came bounding onto the bridge. He was already wearing his temperature control suit. He was obviously psyched to be part of the repair team today.

"Penny, what's up? You aren't dressed for the remote mission," Will said.

Penny groaned. Couldn't Will see how exhausted she was?

"I'm taking Penny's shift today," Judy said, covering for her. "She'll stay on board with Mom and man the command center."

Penny smiled gratefully at Judy. She was in no shape to do any heavy labor.

Penny could hear Major West's strong footsteps going down the hall to the cargo bay. She could hear her father's footsteps following right behind. It was funny the way she could identify people by the sounds of their feet. She figured it came from being with the same people day after day in such a small environment.

A light on the ship's console flashed green. Her father and Major West had entered the cargo bay, probably to load up on tools and supplies they would need for today's mission.

"WILL! PENNY! GET DOWN HERE RIGHT NOW!" Professor Robinson's voice came loudly over the ship's intercom. But he didn't need the intercom. His angry, bellowing voice was loud enough to be heard anywhere in the cosmos.

Penny and Will looked nervously at one another. What had made their father so angry? And how much trouble were they in?

Will walked tentatively down the hallway to the cargo bay. Penny followed close behind, her mind searching for some explanation for their father's anger. She didn't have to wait long to find the reason. As soon as she turned the corner and entered the cargo bay, Penny let out a little gasp. She couldn't believe it! Will had definitely gone too far this time.

The cargo bay was completely covered in a maze of white toilet paper. Every piece of equipment was wrapped in the stuff, and a thick maze of paper hung from the ceilings. As Penny walked through the room, she felt as though she had entered a spiderweb. She batted the paper away from her face and leaned against a pole that had been wrapped like a candy cane.

"Which one of you is responsible for this?" Professor Robinson demanded.

Penny stared at Will. Will stared back at Penny.

"I'm warning whichever one of you is guilty: Your punishment will only be worse if you don't own up to your actions," their father threatened. His face was so red Penny thought he might burst.

Neither Penny nor Will said a word. Penny looked at her feet and kicked at the floor.

"Well, that's it, then. There's only one way to get to the bottom of this. Penny, press the command for a replay of the data stored in the security patrol camera stationed in this cargo bay."

Penny looked sheepishly at Will. She had a feeling the replay of the holographic film from the security camera would show Will hard at work toilet-papering the cargo bay. She didn't want to turn him in, but what could she do? Her father had given her an order.

Penny's father misinterpreted her hesitation. "Is there some reason you don't want us to see the film?" Professor Robinson demanded. "Will we find your image on the replay?"

Penny reluctantly shook her head and pushed a button on the video remote control she carried with her at all times. A small camera overhead made a low whirring sound as its images rewound. Then, with a flick of a second button, the holographic image began to form.

But it wasn't Will. And it wasn't Penny, either. There, in the middle of the room, stood a ghostlike simulation of Robot! Penny watched with surprise as the Robot hologram unraveled roll after roll of toilet paper, hung the sheets from the ceiling and the walls, and then began working on the objects that lined the floor-to-ceiling shelves of the cargo bay. He made toilet paper mummies of the backpacks, tools, emergency lighting gear, and emergency oxygen packs that were stored in the cargo bay.

Penny looked at Will with surprise, and a certain amount of disappointment. It was one thing to try and pull off a stupid trick like this one. It was another thing to get your friend to do the dirty work for you. Robot was not programmed for this kind of stunt. Will must have directed him to do this.

That was exactly what Professor Robinson thought, too. "I don't know what's gotten into you, son, but this has got to stop!" he declared.

"But, Dad, I didn't do . . ." Will interrupted.

Professor Robinson shook his head. "Will, this was the work of your robot. The robot you programmed. This was your handiwork, and now you've got to take your punishment. You are not to have any contact with Robot for one week."

Will was shocked. A whole week without Robot? That seemed like an eternity. Robot was his best friend — his *only* friend — on board the *Jupiter 2*. But Will knew there was no use arguing with his father.

"Now, get this place cleaned up in the next fifteen minutes," Professor Robinson said. "We have no time to waste."

"I'll help him, Dad," Penny volunteered. Suddenly she felt terribly sorry for her brother. She knew how much Robot meant to him.

"Penny, *you* believe me, don't you?" Will asked his sister once their father was gone.

"Look, Will, the stuff you pulled on Dr. Smith was kind of funny," Penny replied. "But this was dumb. You knew the camera would record what was going on."

"But I didn't know what was going on," Will insisted.

Well, if nothing else, her little brother was consistent. "Whatever you say, Will," Penny replied as she began clearing away reams of toilet paper.

As the repair crew was suiting up, Penny took a seat on deck beside her mother.

"Any idea yet about what kind of life-form lives on this planet, Mom?" Penny asked hopefully.

"Well, judging by their footprints, they aren't any larger than you or I," Maureen said. "But I can't get a good grip on anything else. I suspect they are suffering from a lack of vegetation, but I can't even say whether they are carnivores or herbivores."

"I'll keep my fingers crossed for herbivores," Penny replied. She knew that vegetable eaters were usually a lot less threatening than meat eaters. At least they wouldn't be looking to make a meal out of the Robinsons. Of course, Penny knew that even vegetarians could be dangerous — like those two alien beings the Robinsons had brought on board a few months ago. They'd eaten nothing but metal, but they'd still threatened to kill the Robinsons. They'd wanted their bodies to house their children.

47

"You know, Mom, those footprints look like something I've seen before. I just can't place them exactly. But I know that it will come to me," Penny said.

"I don't know where you would have seen them, Penny. This planet was unknown to any earthlings before we landed here. So you wouldn't have seen them in a textbook," Maureen responded.

"I know," Penny said. "That's what's making it so confusing."

"I'll tell you one thing — I like the nightlife a lot better on Earth," Major West joked as he walked onto the bridge. Penny laughed. She suspected that Major West's nightlife at home had included a lot of virtual reality nightclubs where he could dress up and flirt with the ladies, real *and* imagined. These days his nightlife was spent repairing the *Jupiter 2*.

Professor Robinson followed Major West on deck. Will and Judy trailed close behind.

"Will, do as your father says, and don't try any exploring on your own," Mrs. Robinson told Will.

"Don't worry, I'll keep an eye on him," Professor Robinson promised. He looked at Will and added sternly, "I think he'll follow orders today."

Penny watched as her siblings, her father, and Major West prepared to exit the ship. She turned on the video monitors and scanned the planet's surface. There didn't seem to be much of a change. Even the footprints seemed to be intact.

The exit hatch opened. Penny watched the group walk off the ship. Her mom checked their body temperature readings and vital signs. Penny grew nervous when she saw her mother frown.

"There's something wrong with Judy's readings," she told

Penny calmly. "Her weight has suddenly jumped by about ten pounds, and the stress on her muscles is off quite a bit."

Penny watched her mother punch a few number codes into her handheld monitor. She shook her head, and punched in some additional codes.

"Penny, zero in on the repair site," she ordered.

Penny did as she was told. She pushed three buttons, keyed in a number pattern, and watched as the camera projected a holographic image of her sister onto the bridge.

"There! There it is," Penny's mother shouted. "It's inside her supply sack."

Penny studied the sack that was attached to the back of Judy's temperature control suit, sort of like a space backpack. Something had climbed into the sack. And because of its location, Judy couldn't see the slight movement taking place. Some sort of creature was dangerously close to her sister. And if someone didn't warn Judy soon, it might attack her, or worse!

"We've got to warn her," Penny said. She automatically pushed the controls to the ship's external broadcast system.

"That system is still under repair," Penny's mother said. "They can't hear us."

"Then I've got to go down there and warn her," Penny declared.

But her mother had other plans. "No. I am going. This is serious. That could be some sort of life-threatening creature, sweetie. It's my job to check it out."

Penny felt her cheeks flush with nerves. Her father, Will, Judy, and Major West were already on the planet. Now her mother would be there, too. "But that leaves me alone on the ship," she whispered. "Without any communication system to use if I need help in an emergency."

"I won't be long, Pen. And we've got all of the systems stabilized. You won't have to do a thing. And if some little problem does arise, you can handle it, kiddo. I know you can," her mother assured her firmly. "You already know everything you need to. You just have to believe in yourself. If it will make you feel better, I'll leave the emergency hatch slightly open, so you know I can get back on in an instant. And Dr. Smith is still on board. I know that's not much comfort, but I'm sure he would help you if it were a life-or-death situation — especially if it meant *his* life or death."

Penny shook her head. All alone on board the *Jupiter 2* with a homicidal doctor. What a way to spend an evening.

As her mother made her way toward the cargo bay to suit up, Penny remembered her conversation with Will just a day ago. He'd warned her that someday she might be in charge of an entire ship.

Who knew it would be this soon?

8
The Stowaway

Penny sat nervously by the control panel and studied the ship's vital statistics. The oxygen levels seemed normal; the light and alarm systems were activated. Even the temperature readings seemed steady and near normal.

A red light flashed on the console, marking the opening of one of the ship's exits. Penny's mother must have left the ship. Penny sighed. She really was in charge now. The red light flickered on and off. The bouncing light was comforting to Penny — her mother had left the emergency exit ajar, just as she had promised.

Penny adjusted the video camera and followed her mother's footsteps. Then she searched for Judy. But her sister was not with the rest of the repair crew — she'd probably gone off to take some temperature and soil readings for their mother's research. At least, that was what Penny hoped she had done. Penny tried not to think about the other alternatives. She would not let herself think that whatever was inside Judy's backpack had done her older sister any harm.

Bronk! Bronk! Bronk! Penny did not have time to think of any other scenarios. Suddenly the oxygen alarm went off on

51

the bridge. There had been a sudden rise in the amount of oxygen being used on board the *Jupiter 2*, meaning that there was now less oxygen available for each person. And, to make matters worse, at the very same time, due to the open hatch, the temperature levels had risen about ten degrees.

Penny felt a moment of panic. But she was trained for emergencies. She took a deep breath, collected her thoughts, and tried to remain calm. Her first responsibility was to whoever was on board the *Jupiter 2* — which meant Dr. Smith. Much as she hated doing it, Penny had to warn him of the danger.

"Dr. Smith, please put on your temperature control gear and activate your oxygen mask. Come to the bridge immediately. We have an emergency situation. Code Red!"

Penny raced to her cabin and put on her suit and oxygen mask. She searched her room for Blawp. But she could not find the alien anywhere. Quickly Penny tore through her closets and peered under her bed. But the small creature was nowhere to be found.

"Penny Robinson, come to the bridge this instant!" Dr. Smith's voice rang out over the intercom system.

What should she do? The creature could be in great danger — especially with the sudden shift in oxygen and temperature levels.

But Penny knew she had to solve the problem, not search for Blawp. The *Jupiter 2* was in trouble. She made her way to the bridge, hoping the alien had found a way to help herself. After all, Blawp was an extremely self-reliant creature.

"Where have you been?" Dr. Smith cried out to Penny as she walked onto the bridge. "And what have you done to this ship? Where is your mother?"

"Mom is with the away team," Penny stated. "And I am in charge."

Dr. Smith's face went white with fear and then red with anger. "I will not take orders from a teenager," he declared.

Penny stared him down. "I know how this ship works and you don't. You know how much heat and loss of oxygen the human body can stand, and I don't. It seems to me that we work as a team, or we don't survive."

Dr. Smith didn't have any response to that, so Penny went to work activating the emergency systems. She ran a computer check of the oxygen chambers to search for any leakage, but there was none. Still, the level of oxygen being used on board the *Jupiter 2* appeared to have increased dramatically in the past five minutes.

If there was no leakage, that meant someone or something was breathing more than a human's share of oxygen. But almost everyone had left the ship — the oxygen use levels should have gone down, not up.

"There's no leakage," Penny told Dr. Smith. "I can't find any mechanical reason for the oxygen use going up."

"You'll have to find the reason for that later," Dr. Smith said. "Right now, you need to get a larger amount of oxygen onto this ship. Have the computer raise the level of oxygen released into the air."

But Penny couldn't do that without risking a serious decrease in the *Jupiter 2*'s air supply — something they would need while traveling through space. Of course, right now they didn't need a huge supply of oxygen from the ship's systems, because this planet's atmosphere was filled with oxygen, but . . .

Penny nearly jumped out of her seat with excitement. She had the answer. "What we need is some fresh air," she told the doctor. "I'll have to open all of the exit hatches — even the emergency ones."

With a flick of a switch, Penny opened several more exits on the *Jupiter 2*. The increased amount of oxygen in the ship's atmosphere showed up almost immediately on the computer gauge.

But with the additional oxygen came increased heat from the planet's surface.

"You'll have to keep your temperature control suit on for a while, Dr. Smith," Penny said authoritatively. "At least until one of my parents can permanently regulate the systems."

Penny fell limply into her chair and removed her oxygen mask. Taking care of that emergency had taken a lot out of her. She scanned the video cameras in the hope of finding her mother and Judy. Dr. Smith, having no interest in any emergency procedures that did not involve his own safety, returned to his quarters.

It took a while, but finally Penny spotted her mother returning to the repair site. She was carrying her life sciences sample case. Something inside the case was squirming wildly.

Penny saw her mother approach her father. The two spoke briefly. At first her father looked as though he were laughing. Then he looked angry. *What was that all about?* Penny wondered.

Penny watched as her mother reentered the ship. She was still carrying the squirming case. Why was her mother bringing that creature on board? Penny trusted her mother's instincts, but this was definitely taking scientific study too far. Still, Penny was relieved to hear her mother's footsteps approaching the bridge.

"Don't take your temperature control suit off, Mom," Penny warned her mother. "We had a slight emergency while you were away." Quickly Penny explained to her mother about the increased use of oxygen and the higher temperatures.

"That was quick thinking," Mrs. Robinson said. "I'll get on the case right away. But first . . ." She reached over to open her life sciences case.

Penny moved away. She wasn't sure what was about to pop out of there. Her mother reached into the case and pulled out a small, chimplike creature with shiny dragonlike scales.

"Blawp!" Penny reached out and the small alien leaped into her arms. "So that's where you were."

Mrs. Robinson looked stern. "This is no joke, Penny. Blawp stowed away in Judy's pack. She nearly scared me half to death — I was about to call a Code Green, and get your father and Major West involved."

Penny looked at the floor. A Code Green meant capturing an enemy by any means necessary. Judy could have been seriously injured during the procedure.

"You have got to keep track of this creature. That was the condition for you being allowed to keep her on board. I want Blawp placed in an escape-proof cabin. I'll give you special permission to use the energy sources required to put her in a virtual cage. Major West almost has the energy system patched up anyway," her mother ordered.

Penny nodded, and quietly carried her squealing Blawp off the bridge. As they walked down the hall, Penny stared incredulously at the creature. Escaping like that was completely out of character for her. She rarely let Penny out of her sight.

Things on this planet were strange and getting stranger.

9
Robot's Surprise

Penny stayed out of the way when the team returned to the ship. She had a feeling they were all angry at her for letting Blawp run loose.

In actuality, nobody really had time to be angry at Penny. There was major work to be done on the *Jupiter 2*. They had to get to the bottom of the oxygen problem quickly. There was also the matter of the open exits. While everyone agreed that Penny had done a great job of coming up with a temporary solution, it just wasn't safe to leave those doors open. For now, there were robots guarding the exits, and emergency sirens put in place should anyone or any*thing* enter the ship without the proper entry code, but those were anything but foolproof.

Will knocked quietly on Penny's cabin door and walked in. "That was pretty quick thinking, about the oxygen and all," he complimented his sister.

"Thanks," Penny said with more than a little surprise.

"Look, I know you had nothing to do with Blawp sneaking down to the surface in Judy's pack," Will told Penny. "A lot of weird things are happening around here. I'm not the one who played all those jokes on Dr. Smith, and I didn't toilet-paper the cargo bay, either. And even though we saw Robot on that holographic tape, I know that he isn't capable of doing those things, either, because I programmed him all by myself. I haven't been able to program any kind of sense of humor into him. And believe me, it's not for lack of trying. I've moved his wires in every single way, trying to inject humor into his systems.

"But something has gotten into him, and I suspect this planet is the cause," Will added.

Penny looked away. The minute Will mentioned Robot's wiring, she knew she had to tell him about what she had done.

"Uh, Will, about Robot's wiring," Penny began. "I ... well ... you remember those math problems Mom gave us? Well, I had Robot help me with them, and then we had the problem with the new star, and he was in my room, and he kind of got sort of messed up, so I rewired him," Penny admitted in one breath.

Will stared at Penny. "You opened Robot without my permission?" Will screeched. "I can't believe you! That's *my* job. He's *my* Robot! Do I go around messing with your video cameras or your private music system? Who knows what kind of damage you must have done!"

"Do you think I caused him to change his personality like this?" Penny asked nervously.

Will's eyes practically bugged out of his head. He was really angry. The veins in his neck bulged and throbbed and he was breathing heavily. He began screaming scornfully at Penny. "You? Change his personality? No way! You could never do something I couldn't!"

Penny was hurt and angry. But she didn't say a thing. She just stared at Will. She didn't know for sure that she had caused the change in Robot's personality — but did Will know for sure that she hadn't? He thought he was so great. He never allowed for the thought that other people were smart, too.

But it would be a week before Will and Penny would know for certain what had happened to Robot. After all, Will was grounded from being around Robot because of all those practical jokes. He wasn't allowed to open him up and find out.

That afternoon, while everyone was still taking their afternoon nap, Penny sneaked into Will's cabin and woke him up.

"Will, get up," she whispered in his ear.

Will rolled over and stretched. "Is it time to go out again?" he asked through a yawn.

"No," Penny replied. "But I want to help you make sure Robot is okay."

"I'm not allowed to be around Robot," Will said.

"I know. But I am," Penny responded. "So I thought I could focus a holographic camera on Robot and me, and send the image straight to your room. Then you could transmit instructions to me, and I'll fix him up according to your directions."

Will looked at Penny carefully. "First of all, Dad said holographic images are off-limits until we're sure the ship is in perfect shape. Second of all, it's pretty technical work, Pen," Will said slowly. "I don't know if you could handle it."

That did it. Penny was mad now. Really mad.

"Fine," she declared with a toss of her hair. "Forget I offered." She turned and walked out into the hall. She couldn't believe what he had said. She actually was thinking about running back in and punching him when she peered in the doorway and saw him staring sheepishly at the ground. He knew what he had said was really, *really* mean.

"Wait, Pen. Don't go. I think it will work," he said. "I'm sorry I said that."

Penny grinned and stepped back into Will's room. "It won't take that long, and besides, the ship is almost completely fixed. We can make up the energy loss by turning off the lights in my room for a few minutes. We should be able to work with the remote light on my helmet."

Penny raced to the robot bay and brought Robot up to her cabin. Quickly, she fastened a remote holographic transmitter to her wall.

"Will, can you see us?" Penny asked into the camera.

"Yeah. Can you hear me?" Will's voice transmitted into her room.

"Loud and clear. What should I do first?"

"Open up his front panel, and let me take a look," Will said.

Penny did as she was told. "Don't worry, Robot, you won't feel a thing," Penny joked as she used a laser knife to split the seams on Robot's front panel.

"I am not programmed to feel," Robot assured her.

"We're not quite sure what you're programmed for anymore," Penny told him as she focused the camera and the remote light on the internal wiring.

At first, Will didn't say anything. Penny knew that he was busy studying the wiring configurations inside Robot's body. And when Will did speak, his words totally surprised Penny.

"I can't believe what you've done!" Will declared. But he didn't sound angry. He sounded amazed. "I never would have thought of that combination of wiring. Logically, Robot's systems should have completely broken down. Not one law of engineering seems to be working as planned. Penny, you're not going to believe this, but you've turned Robot into a comedian. A real human trait!"

Penny was stunned. "I had no idea what I was doing," she said.

"Maybe not, but it worked," Will declared. "But we can't leave him this way. He's a menace and a threat to the ship. I'll tell you how to rewire him back to normal — as soon as I copy down what you did. Maybe someday I can refine it and give him a sense of humor without the prank element."

Penny waited for Will to make his notes. Then his voice came back over the transmitter. She followed all of his instructions on rewiring Robot's systems. Will was right. The work was far more intricate than she had ever imagined. And more than once she slipped up. But Will was patient, and talked her through the whole thing.

Finally, the wiring was complete. She sealed up Robot's front panel and helped him to his feet. The lights in Robot's head began to flash as he ran a check of his functioning systems.

"Repairs completed," Robot reported to Will.

"Let's just make sure," Will told him. "Explain to me the simplest way to short-sheet a bed."

Lights flashed on and off in Robot's head. "I have no record of the action of short-sheeting in my memory bank," Robot declared.

"That should do it," Will said. "Good job, Penny."

Penny grinned. "We make a pretty good team when we want to, little bro," she said. She was about to sign off with Will when suddenly she heard a series of loud blawping noises coming from the lower cargo bay, a small storage area located just below the main cargo bay that Robot had toilet-papered. The lower cargo bay was dark and cold. The Robinsons used the space to store extra tools. The backup computer memory bank was also kept in the lower cargo bay because it had to be stored in a cool spot.

It wouldn't make any sense for Blawp to go there. She was afraid of the dark.

Blawp's sounds were more high-pitched and squeaky than those that Penny was used to hearing, but they were undeniably the sounds of Blawp. And if Blawp was loud before, now the creature seemed totally out of control. She sounded like a whole herd of blawps instead of just one!

But Penny had locked Blawp up in a soundproof virtual cage. The cage was escape-proof. There was no way Blawp could have gotten loose and ended up in the lower cargo bay. Or was there?

"Will, meet me in the lower cargo bay, quick!" Penny shouted to her brother. "I think Blawp may be in danger."

10
The Nest

Will and Penny raced down to the lower cargo bay as fast as they could. The closer they got, the louder the blawping became.

It wasn't easy to reach the lower cargo bay. They had to go through the upper cargo bay, move several storage canisters, and climb through a small opening. But Penny was determined to get to Blawp.

"Hurry up, Will," Penny shouted over the din. "We've got to get Blawp back in that cage before she wakes up Mom and Dad. We heard the noises first because we were awake, but it won't be long before the others register what's going on here. And if they find out that Blawp has gotten loose again, they'll be super mad."

Will nodded. Penny knew he would help her. She'd just helped him — and that meant he owed her one. Quickly, Will got to work moving the heavy canisters out of the way so they could enter the lower cargo bay.

"Oh my gosh!" Penny exclaimed as she climbed through the small opening. She couldn't believe her eyes. Instead of a room filled with large steel canisters and a computer memory bank, Penny discovered what looked like a high-tech log cabin made out of canisters stacked one on top of the other. She had never seen anything like it.

The blawping seemed to be coming from inside the structure. Blawp was obviously inside. But how had she gotten there? She couldn't have moved those canisters on her own. Was there another creature on board? Some sort of monster who had kidnapped her? Penny wanted to rescue Blawp as quickly as possible, but Will held her back.

"Blawp obviously didn't do this," Will said simply. "And we don't know what kind of creature did. This is not something we can handle on our own."

Penny could feel her stomach sink. Will wasn't a coward. Usually he was quick to explore and solve problems on his own. If he was frightened, he had good reason to be. Penny was going to have to wake her parents, and let the chips fall where they may. Even though she had taken plenty of precautions, somehow Blawp had gotten loose again. Reluctantly she contacted her folks through her portable intercom system.

Before they responded, Penny could hear them heading for the lower cargo bay. Blawp had taken care of waking them for her. In fact, Blawp had not just woken Penny's mom and dad, she'd woken up Judy, Major West, and Dr. Smith as well. Penny raced to the upper cargo bay to meet them.

"Penny, I thought I told you to lock Blawp up," Mrs. Robinson moaned as she rubbed the sleep from her eyes.

Dr. Smith angrily agreed. "There is not enough room on this ship for that horrible creature and me!" he declared. "There isn't enough room in this *universe*!"

"Don't tempt me, Smith," Major West said. Even when he

was half awake, the major had the ability to pick on Dr. Smith. He yawned and looked at Penny. "I've got to tell you, though, kiddo, this is getting to me, too."

"I'm disappointed, Penny," Judy added. "This is not the responsible care I thought you were capable of."

"I wouldn't speak of responsibility if I were you," Dr. Smith told Judy. "I believe you were the one to bring the little monster on board, Dr. Robinson. Now see what a mess that caused!"

"How dare you!" Judy replied, glaring at Dr. Smith.

Penny looked into the eyes of her shipmates. She wanted to tell them that none of this was anyone's fault. Blawp had just escaped. But she knew they wouldn't believe her.

Will came to his sister's defense. "Look, you guys," he said, "Penny *did* lock up Blawp. I saw her do it. But somehow she got loose. And now she's being held prisoner in a — well, there's no way to describe it. You'll have to see it for yourself." Will moved out of the way and let the family down below. They gasped when they saw the cabinlike structure in the center of the room.

"Who did this?" Professor Robinson demanded. "Will, if this is another of Robot's tricks . . ."

"It's not, Dad, I promise. We don't know who did it," Penny said. "That's why we called you."

"There's only one way to find out what's going on here," Major West said. He flexed his muscles and began to move the canisters. When he'd cleared away enough to make a small opening, he peered inside. "You guys are never going to believe this. Penny, come here and take a peek."

Penny walked tentatively up to Major West. Will followed close behind.

Penny stared at the canisters in disbelief. There, inside the cabin, was a nest made of wire — wire that had obviously been removed from the backup computer memory bank. Inside the nest were four tiny Blawps, about the size of Chihuahuas.

"Where did you guys come from?" Penny asked the little creatures as she stared into their eyes.

"We'd better not let them escape," Will said.

Penny sighed. That was Will. Ever logical.

"I'll put them in a virtual cage for now," Will said. He reached in to grab one of the tiny Blawps. But before he could get his hands on one, he heard a familiar voice.

"Danger, Will Robinson," Robot warned. "Danger!"

11
The Planet of the Blawps

The sound of Robot's warning caused Will to turn around rapidly. Suddenly four huge creatures darted into the lower cargo bay of the *Jupiter 2*. They were about the size of human females, with large, lumpy bodies that were covered with bumps. Their skin was yellow and scaly, and like Penny's Blawp, they appeared to be able to change skin color like a chameleon. At first Penny didn't know what they were. Then she heard them blawping wildly. These were adult Blawps! And right now, they were heading straight for Will!

Will dodged a leaping Blawp. "What's going on?" he shouted.

"I think they're trying to protect their young," Mrs. Robinson answered. "I'd move away from those babies if I were you," she told her son.

Will moved away from the nest. But it was too late. The larger Blawps now viewed him as the enemy. And they were determined to move him out of the cargo bay.

It was four against one. Penny knew that Blawps were usually docile creatures, but when they were provoked they could cause trouble. Penny had seen that in action when the *Jupiter*

2 had been invaded by the metal-eating aliens. Penny's Blawp had attacked the aliens when they had tried to hurt Penny. If these Blawps thought Will had tried to injure their young, her brother was in trouble!

A large Blawp made a quick jump toward Will, its claws poised for attack. Will hopped out of the way just in time.

Penny knew he needed help. She called to her own Blawp, hoping that she would come and call off these big Blawps. But Penny's Blawp did not reply. She couldn't, Penny realized. She was still held prisoner in the soundproof holographic cage. She hadn't escaped after all.

That gave Penny an idea. Quickly she pushed a button on her portable handheld computer and created an impenetrable invisible wall.

"Quick, Will, into the cage," she shouted to her brother as she pointed in the direction of the wall.

"The what?" Will began. But he stopped in midsentence, realizing Penny was right. The virtual cage would protect him from the Blawps.

Will leaped in the direction Penny had pointed. Penny looked at her handheld computer, noted when Will was in the correct position, and created a small opening in the wall. She sealed the opening quickly, before the Blawps could follow Will in. Then she pushed a three-button code into a portable locking system, and the invisible shelter was sealed.

The Blawps reached for Will but were repelled by the invisible wall. After a few tries, they were satisfied that their children were safe from big bad Will. The four of them went over to the computer wire nest to console their squawking babies.

"I guess I owe you an apology, Penny," Judy said.

"I think we all do," her mother added, putting her arm around Penny's shoulders.

"That's okay," Penny said. "At least we know why the oxygen levels seemed so off. Those new Blawps used an awful lot of oxygen." She looked at the four bigger Blawps carefully holding their babies. Then she looked at the nest of wires from the backup computer memory bank.

"You guys sure have your work cut out for you untangling that mess," Penny added. "I wish I knew how all of these Blawps wound up here."

"Well, I suspect we started with those big ones," Mrs. Robinson said. "The little ones in the nest must have been born in the past day or so."

"Okay, so where did those four big ones come from?" Penny adjusted her query.

Will waved his hands inside his holographic soundproof cage to get his family's attention. Penny looked at him and laughed. He looked like a wild man.

"You know, I think I like him this way." But she pushed another button on the portable system and removed the soundproofing.

"I just had an amazing thought," Will volunteered.

Penny groaned. Modesty was certainly not Will's strong suit.

"Maybe this is the Blawps' home planet. I mean, Robot did say that Penny's Blawp was trying to communicate with someone. And the only creatures who would understand Blawp's language would be other Blawps. What if Penny's Blawp was sort of like a whale who had been separated from her pod? And as we got closer to the planet, Blawp could hear her own language. It makes sense that she would call out, doesn't it?"

Penny stared at Will. The kid was really amazing. He could put facts together like no one else. And usually his theories were correct. *Usually.*

"But Will, we know the Blawps built a sophisticated space-ship. Why would their home planet be so barren, with no shelter, no evidence of civilization or anything?"

"Well, it's possible they traveled here from their home planet, trying to escape unsafe living conditions."

"I guess that's possible," Penny agreed. But she still had a few questions for her mother. "This planet has very little water or vegetation, right, Mom?" Penny asked her mother. Mrs. Robinson nodded. "And I know that Blawps like bananas, and apples, and oranges," Penny continued. "And they do drink some water. So why would they choose to land on a dry, desertlike planet like this one?"

Her mother shook her head. "You're assuming that this planet has been in a desert state for centuries now. But remember, my tests showed that the planet had only been hot and dry for a short while. My guess is that the creation of that new star has changed the atmosphere here drastically. The Blawps were unprepared for it, so when they came across the *Jupiter 2*, they must have decided to search out a cool, comfortable place to bear their young."

Will smiled triumphantly. His mother had completely backed up his theory. "I'm not sure where the adult Blawps got their water supply on board, but I suspect that when we take a reading, we'll find a slight unexpected drop in the water supply."

"But how did they get on board the *Jupiter 2*? We've got robot guards and alarms at every entrance and exit. One of those would have notified us," Penny said.

"Wait a minute, Penny, you're forgetting something — those guards have only been in place since the drop in oxygen forced us to leave the doors open. But what about that first day we were on the surface? They could have sneaked on board through one of the holes in the ship's exterior. That's the way those footprints were facing," Mrs. Robinson said.

The footprints! Now Penny knew why the footprints looked so familiar. Their three-toed pattern matched Blawp's feet perfectly. *Oh!* If Penny had just made the connection earlier, she would have saved the family so much aggravation. But the truth was, Penny didn't really care how or when the Blawps came on board the *Jupiter 2*. She was just glad they had. And she was glad that the babies had been born in an atmosphere in which they could survive.

She looked down at the babies. They were adorable. But what were the odds that four of them would have been born on the exact same day? How long had the older Blawps been pregnant? Judy had said that Blawps were a self-replicating species. So what had caused all these Blawps to replicate at the exact same time?

Judy must have been thinking the same thing, because she remarked, "I'd like to take a look at those older Blawps, and their babies, too. Perhaps some change on the planet's surface caused them to replicate at the exact same moment. Penny, if you don't mind, I'd like to compare the physical states of the Blawps who have just had babies with your Blawp, since she's not pregnant. Maybe we can figure out what's going on on this planet."

"I'd hurry if I were you, Judy," Will said. "If these four Blawps have come on board to give birth, it may mean that their planet is no longer hospitable to them as a species. And that could mean the end of the Blawps as a species forever."

Penny gasped. That couldn't be true. She prayed that Will was wrong. But as Penny and the others knew, Will's theories were almost never wrong. There was no time to waste.

"I'll go get Blawp," Penny told the others. She raced off the bridge toward the holographic cage. As she ran into the image room, she found Blawp just as she'd left her, inside the cage, still wailing. Penny released the holographic image, and Blawp leaped in the air, running in the direction of the bridge. Penny followed close behind. She was so busy watching Blawp that she practically tripped over a big Blawp that was lying in the middle of the hall.

The big Blawp looked exactly like the other adult Blawps, except that her back was swollen in a large hump, as though she were a hunchbacked Blawp. She lay on the floor on her side. Beads of perspiration formed on her shiny skin. Penny's Blawp leaped up and down beside the big Blawp, probably shrieking for help.

"Judy! Judy! Come here," Penny cried into her intercom pager. "I've found a big Blawp, and I think she's really sick."

12
Newborn Blawp

It seemed to Penny that it took forever for Judy to make her way from the lower cargo bay to the passageway near Penny's cabin, but it really took no more than a minute.

Judy took one look at the warm, sweating Blawp and pulled out her holographic medical scanner. She expertly ran the scanner over the adult Blawp's body. Holographic images of the Blawp's inner organs appeared. Blood and temperature readings registered on the scanner. Judy studied the results for a moment, shook her head, and then ran the scanner over the Blawp's body for a second time. Then she grinned.

"We're about to meet a new Blawp," Judy said joyfully.

Penny looked curiously at Judy. What was she talking about?

"This Blawp is about to become a mother," Judy went on. "And a father. That's the joy of self-replicating — two parents for the price of one!"

Penny was overjoyed. "Wow, now you can compare the pregnant Blawp with the ones that just had babies, and with the one that's been on board with us. Maybe that will give you some insight into what's causing them all to reproduce at once."

"You're beginning to think like a real scientist, Pen," Judy complimented her. "After just running these few preliminary tests, I think I know what causes the Blawps to replicate. Judging by the air temperature on the planet, and by comparing the body temperature of your Blawp and this Blawp, I can make an educated guess as to what has brought on this Blawp baby boom. I suspect that the elevated temperature on the Blawps' planet initiated the reproductive process in the Blawps. And the hotter it gets on that planet, the more Blawps will be born."

"But Judy, that's terrible!" Penny exclaimed. "As it is, the planet has almost no food or water available anymore. If they were to have a population explosion, most of the Blawps would die!"

Judy nodded gravely. "Right now, we just have to take care of this Blawp. We'll have to provide it with a good place for its nest — and some material to make it with."

Penny knew just the place. She helped the Blawp to her feet and led her to the cargo bay, where she provided her with tons of toilet paper for her nest — the very paper Robot had used in his infamous practical joke.

The baby Blawp was born safely within the hour. The baby's bright blue eyes seemed huge in her tiny face, and her shiny scales were changing color rapidly, like an old-fashioned kaleidoscope, as her camouflage ability developed. Penny brought her Blawp to see the new baby — she knew Blawp hadn't seen a baby of its own species since it had wound up on board the *Jupiter 2*.

But Blawp did not seem particularly interested in the baby. She was just happy to be out of the cage. Which reminded Penny — she was the one who held the key to Will's cage. He was still locked in there, safe from the angry Blawps. But the four big Blawps seemed content with their rapidly developing infants, and posed little danger now. In fact, the lower cargo bay sounded like a Blawp nursery, with the adult Blawps cooing to the younger Blawps, and the younger Blawps letting out little high-pitched blawping squeaks in response.

"Okay, bro, freedom time," Penny told Will as she pulled out the portable locking system and began to enter the code.

"It's about time," Will said. "I've been in here for hours, and those Blawps won't shut up."

Penny sighed. Will was so ungrateful. She'd saved his life, and here he was complaining. Well, Penny knew how to fix that! She pushed a button, and the sound of Will's voice disappeared.

Ah, the joys of soundproofing!

Penny was about to leave the bridge when her parents arrived to do some work on the computer's backup memory bank.

"Oh, good, I see you're going to let Will out now," her mother said with a knowing look.

Well, that wasn't exactly what Penny had had in mind, but now that she'd been caught, she reached down and punched in the code that unlocked the cage. The cage disappeared, and Will stood tall for the first time in several hours.

"Very funny, Penny," Will said sarcastically.

"Will, you just missed it. This big Blawp had a baby — right in the cargo bay! Now Blawp and baby are both resting comfortably," Penny told her brother.

Will looked shocked — and more than a little disappointed. Penny could tell that he was upset to have missed a life sciences experience. The birth of a Blawp was something he could have recorded in his computer bank of knowledge.

"The baby is so cute," Penny continued. "They all are. I wish we could keep all the Blawps here on board with us. That way they would be safe. Their planet isn't fit for their life-form anymore."

Just then Dr. Smith entered the lower cargo bay. "Keep them all on board? I refuse to go traveling through space in the middle of a floating zoo! Imagine the kind of danger these creatures will put us in. They've already all but destroyed our oxygen system. What's next — the food supply?"

Professor Robinson looked up from his work on the backup system and frowned. "He's right, Penny," he said slowly.

Penny gulped. Her dad agreeing with Dr. Smith? This was not good.

"It's hard to concentrate with all that blawping going on," Professor Robinson continued. "And rewiring this system is very delicate work."

"Too bad there's not enough room in the image room for all of them," Will said. "We could put them in my soundproof music room."

"Yeah," Penny agreed. Then she had a thought. "Hey, Will, didn't you say you were learning to play the drums?"

Will nodded.

"And Mom, you play a little guitar, don't you?"

Mrs. Robinson looked confused. "It's been a long time since I picked one up," she admitted. "Why?"

"Because we are going to help these Blawps get a little shut-eye. We're going to sing to them," Penny announced.

Dr. Smith rolled his eyes upward. "As if I didn't have to put up with enough noise," he moaned.

"Oh, but Dr. Smith, you're going to sing harmonies," Penny said sweetly. "We need all the help we can get."

Dr. Smith pulled on his goatee and sighed. But he followed Penny, Will, and Maureen up to the holographic image room.

There was not enough space in the image room for all eleven Blawps, so Will opened one end of it so the Blawps could hear the music. Penny had to admit that the word "music" was being used loosely. Will's drumming was not always on the beat, her mom's guitar chops were a little rusty, and Dr. Smith stood nearby with a scowl on his face as Penny tried to sing in tune.

But somehow the Blawps seemed soothed by their songs. Maybe they were just tired. Or maybe they were going to sleep in self-defense, to block out the cacophony. Whatever the case, the Blawps finally fell asleep.

"Well, that problem's solved," Penny said proudly.

"For now," Will agreed. "But the minute one of those babies opens its mouth, they're all going to get up. And this will start all over again. We've got to come up with a more permanent solution."

Will was right. The question was, what kind of solution could the crew of the *Jupiter 2* come up with? And would they come up with it in time to save the planet of the Blawps?

13
The Blawps Revolt!

As Professor Robinson and Major West continued their work on the backup computer memory bank, Maureen, Judy, Penny, and Will met to discuss a solution to the Blawp problem. Everyone was in agreement — the Blawps could not stay on board the *Jupiter 2* much longer. As Dr. Smith had so angrily predicted, the food supply was already lower than budgeted for, especially when it came to the fruit and vegetable food packs that the Blawps so eagerly inhaled on an almost hourly basis.

There was also the issue of the rapid reproduction process of the Blawps. If Judy's research proved true and heat did speed up the Blawps' reproductive process, then the longer the ship's doors remained open, the more chance the Blawps had of being exposed to the warm air on the planet's surface. And although the crew had discovered the reason for the change in oxygen levels, they could not afford to increase the amount of oxygen on board until after they were sure that the backup memory bank would not fail in an emergency. Unlike the crew of the *Jupiter 2*, the Blawps were not in temperature control suits. All that warmth would surely bring on another series of Blawp births. In fact, there were three more new Blawps by the time the week was out.

There was no doubt about it. The Blawps would have to return to their planet.

"My preliminary tests do show some underground springs," Mrs. Robinson reported. "In fact, I noticed some shallow wells dug into the planet's surface. They may have been built by the Blawps in an attempt to reach water. But they obviously didn't have the tools necessary to drill through the planet's thick, rocky surface."

"Maybe we can use a laser drill to break through the surface to the water source and create a well for the Blawps," Penny suggested.

Will shook his head. "That won't work, Penny. The water would eventually evaporate in this intense heat. And the Blawps would be back to square one."

"According to my calculations, it would take about fifty years for all the water in the underground sources to completely evaporate, should the situation remain exactly the same as it is today," Mrs. Robinson said matter-of-factly.

"Then the water would buy them some time," Judy countered. "And the Blawps are a pretty smart civilization. After all, they managed to build the ship that was attached to the *Proteus*, didn't they?"

Will and Penny nodded.

"Surely in the next fifty years they can find their own solution to this problem," Judy continued.

Penny looked at the floor. She knew the Blawps could not stay on board the *Jupiter 2*. This was their only shot. Quickly, she volunteered to be part of the team that would drill to the nearest underwater spring. Judy agreed to join her.

Penny and Judy left the *Jupiter 2* for the planet's surface just before dark. They took with them two powerful laser drill bits, which would literally burn a huge well into the planet's surface. The laser was dangerous — one slip and Judy and Penny could be disintegrated along with the planet's rocky surface.

But Penny was surprisingly calm as she and Judy set the drill above the space where the Blawps had built their first wells. She was not thinking about herself. She was thinking about the survival of the Blawps.

As soon as the laser drill was in place, Penny and Judy checked the surrounding area for any Blawps. They did not want to hurt any of the planet's inhabitants during the blast. But the planet seemed eerily empty — as if all of the Blawps other than the ones on board the *Jupiter 2* were already dead. Of course, they could have been hiding in some of the cooler caves, or on another part of the planet. That thought gave Penny some comfort.

Judy made a final check of all the controls on the laser drill. Then she signaled to Penny, who followed her to an area behind a tall rock and set up a lead shield.

"We should be safe here," Judy told Penny. "Barring any sudden shifts in the land formations, the laser should shoot straight down."

Penny knew that Judy was referring to earthquakes or volcanic eruptions. Luckily, the ship's computer had reported that the underground spring was in a very stable section of the planet.

"Just promise me that from the second I activate the drill, you will look away. Even with your protective sun shield, the light from this drill could cause permanent damage to your eyes," Judy ordered.

Penny nodded. Then she bent down below the lead shield and waited for Judy's signal.

"Okay, begin the countdown," Judy told Penny.

Penny crossed her fingers for luck, looked down toward the ground, and began counting backward from ten. When she reached the number one, Penny heard Judy activate the drill. She watched as her sister followed the laser's progress on a small remote screen attached to her wrist. When the screen indicated that the laser had reached the spring, Judy deactivated it.

"Okay, let's see what we've got," Judy said.

Penny stood and followed her sister to the digging site. Penny was afraid to look. If this didn't work, the Blawps were in big trouble. Finally she peeked over Judy's shoulder and sighed with relief. There was a brand-new well filled with fresh water.

"Mmmm. That looks good," Penny said, bending over to take a sip of the cool liquid.

"Oh, no, you don't," Judy stopped her. "We don't know what that water is made of. It may not be the H_2O we're used to. It could be dangerous to non-Blawps."

"But I'll bet the Blawps will be happy to have some," Penny said as she scooped up some Blawp water and placed it in one of her mother's sampling vials.

Penny was so happy she practically skipped up to the bridge of the *Jupiter 2*. "Hi there!" she greeted the visiting Blawps. "Guess what. You've got water now. You can go home!" Penny knew the Blawps could not understand her words, but she was certain that her enthusiasm transcended language.

"Good job, you two," Maureen congratulated her daughters as she joined them on the bridge. "Did you bring me a sample for testing?"

Penny proudly handed her mother the vial of cool liquid. "Mission accomplished," she said.

Just then Dr. Smith came running onto the bridge. Behind him were two baby Blawps. One baby hopped onto his shoulder and started pulling at his hair. The other wrapped itself around his leg.

"Are we able to send these miniature monsters back to where they came from yet?" Dr. Smith demanded.

"Oh, they just want to play," Penny explained. But Dr. Smith was not amused.

"Actually, we can start transporting the Blawps onto the planet right now," Judy said. "We just have to round them all up."

"I know how to do that," Penny said. "Just open up a packet of bananas. They'll follow that anywhere."

Mrs. Robinson went down toward the galley and came back with three large food packets of bananas. She opened the packets and placed them at the exit ramp that led to the planet's surface. Sure enough, all of the Blawps came running — even Penny's Blawp!

Suddenly, Penny's mood dropped. It had never occurred to her that her own Blawp would want to return to her home planet. Penny was faced with the reality that this creature — which she often thought of as a pet — was actually an intelligent life-form, and part of her own civilization. Blawp had her own mind, and she would have to follow her own heart. Would Blawp choose to stay on board the *Jupiter 2* with Penny — or return home?

Penny watched as her Blawp followed the others toward the food. But just as the pack of Blawps were about to take the food and exit the *Jupiter 2*, the largest one let out a deep soulful cry. Then she turned and stormed back onto the *Jupiter 2*. Quickly the other Blawps lifted their young and followed.

"Come on, you guys, it's your home, go ahead," Penny coaxed.

But the Blawps started to howl. *"BLOOOOOP! BLAWWWWWWP! BLAWWWWP!"*

The noise was almost deafening.

Professor Robinson and Major West left their places at the computer console and came racing down toward the open ramp.

"What's going on down here?" Professor Robinson demanded.

"The Blawps just won't leave, Dad," Penny explained.

"We'll see about that," Dr. Smith remarked. Obviously the doctor was really sick of all the Blawps, because he actually took some action. He grabbed the largest Blawp by the arm and tried dragging her down the ramp. The big Blawp freed her limb and raced back up the ramp, knocking the doctor to the floor.

The Blawps leaped up onto computer consoles and high shelves, and even tried hanging from overhead lights, anything to get out of the reach of the crew of the *Jupiter 2*.

Crash! Penny leaped out of the way just as a box of halogen bulbs came flying down off a shelf. The Blawp that was sitting on the shelf leaped down onto the ground and ran toward the robot bay. A baby Blawp leaped after the bigger one. But the baby was slower than the adult and Penny was able to capture her and hold her tightly in her arms.

"Don't you go near my robots!" Will screamed at the big Blawp as he ran toward the robot bay.

The little Blawp twisted and turned in Penny's arms. But Penny held tight. She looked up at the group of frightened Blawps overhead and sighed nervously. One thing was for sure. She didn't have to worry about her Blawp leaving the ship. At least not right now. It seemed that none of the Blawps were leaving the *Jupiter 2* until their safety was better assured.

But how was the crew of the *Jupiter 2* supposed to arrange that?

Penny went back to her cabin and flopped down on her bed. The whole Blawp experience was becoming very frustrating. Sometimes being up in space with her family made Penny feel excited and important. But at times like these, Penny just wished she were back on Earth having normal teenage problems like bad hair days.

Penny stood up and looked in her mirror. This would definitely be one of those bad hair days, she thought. Between the two-minute showers and the temperature control helmets, her hair was probably a flat mess. Penny had to laugh as she looked at her baggy metallic suit with the temperature control pad on the sleeve. Not exactly high-fashion. And definitely not the kind of thing you'd find in a virtual fashion environment.

Suddenly Penny was struck by the shallowness of her vanity. Why should she be worrying about her hair when the Blawps were worrying about survival? Penny made a silent vow to stop looking in the mirror so frequently. There had to be a better way to use a piece of shiny glass.

And that was when Penny's big idea hit her. Mirrors. Indoor environments.

"Mom! Dad!" Penny cried out. "I've got it! I know how we can save the Blawps!"

14
Penny's Plan

Penny raced up to the bridge. She was glad to discover that Major West, Will, and Judy were all there with her parents.

"I've got it! I've got it!" Penny said between deep breaths.

"Whoa! Slow down," Professor Robinson said. "Got what?"

"A plan to save the Blawps," Penny said. "Will, let me know if this is going to work, okay?"

Will looked at his sister with amazement. Penny wasn't always this confident. And she wasn't always so eager to ask his opinion.

"I was sitting in my room, looking in the mirror, thinking about an indoor fashion environment," Penny began. She ignored the mocking look Will shot at her and just kept talking. "And that's when it hit me. If we could build an indoor environment for the Blawps, they could live in there, out of their planet's sun's rays."

"I don't think so, Penny," Will interjected. "The sun is very strong here. No matter how thick we made the stone walls, the heat would penetrate."

Penny shook her head. "I wasn't finished yet, Will," she

scolded him. "I don't think we should build the structure from stone. At least, not completely . . ."

Will interrupted his sister once again. "But that's the only material available on the planet," he said.

"Who said we were going to use material from the planet?" Penny countered. "Do you remember when we used the reflective shields to ward off all of the heat from the new star when we were being pulled into its orbit? Well, I was thinking — if we used mirrors, shiny tile, and other extremely reflective sources to cover the outside of the environment, we'd be able to ward off the heat inside."

At first everyone was silent. Penny could tell they were allowing her plan to register — and thinking of reasons the scenario would not work. Finally, it was Will who said something.

"It could work, Penny," he said. "It's as good as any plan I could come up with."

Penny scowled. Talk about a backhanded compliment. But there was no time to deal with Will now. They would have to get moving if they wanted to build that environment before there was another Blawp baby boom. Although Penny's father and Major West were certain they would have the problem with the oxygen system fixed within a day, the heat from the open doors was already causing some of the Blawps to look unusually large — indicating that they were in the process of self-replicating once again.

"Okay, Penny, since this is your project, what do you think we should do first?" Penny's dad asked.

Penny was shocked. Her father was giving her command of the Blawp plan? *Whoa!*

"Well, I guess Will should gather as many robots as he can to start building the initial stone structure," Penny said. "Judy and I can start removing most of the mirrors — we only need one big one that we can all share in the bathroom." Penny did not even acknowledge the looks of surprise her family gave her. She knew that she was growing up. Maybe after this, they would realize it, too.

"Then we all have to pitch in and get this thing built quickly," Penny concluded. "I think we're about to be overrun by Blawps." As if on cue, two baby Blawps came scampering onto the bridge. One jumped up on the computer console and began pushing buttons. *BRONK!* The emergency signal blared.

"Let's get moving, everyone," Professor Robinson said as he hurried to turn off the alarm system.

Building the Blawps' environment did not prove to be as easy as it seemed. Excavating the stone from the planet's surface could be done rather quickly, thanks to the laser drills on board the *Jupiter 2*. And there were plenty of building tools and supplies on board the ship from the Robinsons' original mission, which would have required building shelters on Alpha Prime. But computing the optimum shape for the structure was no simple task. Robot completed several plans, but many of them required weeks — even years — to build. And every day there seemed to be a new baby Blawp on the *Jupiter 2*. Finally the family settled on a long, wide-roofed plan that could be constructed with thick, mortarlike bricks. The environment stretched as long as six city blocks.

When the time came to enclose the structure in reflective material, Penny spent hours polishing tiles and mirrors, and gathering strips of aluminum foil and scraps from the hems of metallic space suits. Finally she had enough material to cover the entire building.

Penny knew she would never forget the feeling of success when she walked into the enclosed environment for the very first time. The room was cool, and the artificial lighting Will had rigged up gave the place a twilight kind of feel. Water flowed from a spring in the middle of the area. Maureen had suggested planting seeds from the few plants still alive on the planet, and transplanting the live plants into the environment. The plants had been placed directly under the lights to help them grow. Already a few fruits and berries had begun to sprout. Deep in her heart, Penny knew that the Blawps were going to survive.

But Penny also knew that the Blawps were going to have to make some changes in their lifestyle if they were to survive inside the enclosed environment. It would best serve their purposes to sleep inside during the daylight hours, and to go out onto the planet's surface at night, just as the crew had done during their stay on the overheated planet. The air would be cooler then, and the Blawps could go about their usual business. It would take some adjustment from the older Blawps, but knowing what she did about evolutionary theories, Penny predicted that in a couple of hundred generations, the Blawps would develop into a nocturnal species.

"Well, this is it," Penny said to her parents. "It's time to introduce the Blawps to their new home."

"So, how are we going to do that, Penny?" her mother asked.

Penny frowned. This leader thing was getting a bit tough. It was already quite clear that the Blawps weren't particularly willing to leave the safety and security of the *Jupiter 2* for an unknown area. And even though the environment perfectly suited their needs, Penny wasn't quite sure how to communicate the idea to the Blawps. They were an incredibly bright species, but they didn't speak English. And the computer of the *Jupiter 2* could not translate their speech patterns.

The only thing Penny knew for sure was that the Blawps could speak to one another. And that gave her another great idea!

15
Saying Good-bye

"Be right back you guys," Penny called as she ran out of the new Blawp environment and onto the *Jupiter 2*. She headed straight for her cabin, where she was certain she would find her original Blawp.

Sure enough, Penny found her sitting on her bed, sneaking a bite of Penny's secret chocolate stash.

"Hey! What are you doing?" Penny asked. Blawp continued happily chewing. Penny had to laugh. She scooped the creature into her arms. "Come here, you've got a job to do," she told her.

Penny carried Blawp down the corridor to the ramp that led to the new environment. She walked over to her waiting family, and put Blawp down on the ground.

Blawp sniffed around for a while, and then took a big sip of water from the spring.

"*Blawp! Blawp! Bloop!*" Blawp began making high-pitched noises. Then she stopped as if waiting for a response.

"*Blawp! Bloop! Bloop!*" Blawp called out again.

Almost instantly, Penny heard the sound of Blawp footsteps coming down the ramp. All right! Penny's plan had worked.

Blawp had called to the others. Now they were all coming to the environment.

There were eleven big Blawps in all, and countless babies. Penny watched with excitement as they walked around their new environment, examining the water sources and tentatively picking at the berries that had begun growing on the transplanted bushes and shrubs.

Then one of the adult Blawps did a very curious thing. She began picking off some of the drier branches and placing them in a pile.

"Hey! Don't kill those plants . . ." Penny began shouting. But her mother stopped her.

"The Blawp's not killing the plants, honey," Mrs. Robinson said. "She's building a nest. That Blawp has decided that this place is home."

The Robinsons breathed a collective sigh of relief.

"And now we have to get back to our home, at least our home for now," Mrs. Robinson said, indicating the *Jupiter 2*. "Our work here is done."

Penny watched as her family headed back toward the *Jupiter 2*. Then she looked at her Blawp. She was blawping and playing happily among her own kind.

"Just a minute, Mom," Penny said with a shaky voice. "I want to say good-bye."

Penny walked over to Blawp, who was busy eating an oversized blueberry. Penny gave her a hug, and then wiped away a tear.

Penny knew she would miss Blawp a lot. But she understood why the creature would want to live among her own species. Penny fought the urge to look back one more time. Slowly she boarded the *Jupiter 2* and joined the rest of the crew on the bridge.

"You did it, Penny! You saved them," Will said.

Penny was shocked. That was a full compliment, with no ifs, ands, or buts attached! But Penny was too sad to rejoice.

"Everyone is on board now, Dad. We can go when you're ready," Penny said as she reported in.

"*Blawp! Bloop! Bloop! Blawp!*"

Penny couldn't believe her ears. The blawping seemed to be coming from outside the hatch.

"Something's wrong!" Penny said immediately. "That Blawp sounds desperate."

"That's what happens when you leave a teenager in charge," Dr. Smith insisted. "But I think we've done all we can for those creatures. We cannot waste another millisecond on them."

Penny felt her face getting red. Part of her was furious at Dr. Smith for wanting to abandon the Blawps. And part of her was angry at herself, because Dr. Smith was obviously correct. She'd messed up. And the Blawps were going to suffer for her mistakes.

"Open the hatch, Major West," Professor Robinson ordered quietly. He walked over to Penny and put his arm around her as Major West pushed the remote button. As the hatch opened, Penny and her father approached it together.

Thwap! A small Blawp leaped into Penny's arms, and grabbed her tightly around the neck. It was Blawp, her outer space pal! She wanted to stay with Penny. There had been no problem with the Blawp environment, after all. Everything had gone exactly as planned!

"Oh, no! Not again," Dr. Smith moaned. "That overgrown lizard isn't staying, is it?"

"She sure is," Penny declared happily.

"Prepare for takeoff," Professor Robinson told the crew of the *Jupiter 2*. "Let's continue this mission!"

As the Robinsons and Dr. Smith took their seats, Robot wheeled himself over to Dr. Smith.

"Do you know what some creatures would say about this, Doctor?" he asked.

"What?" Dr. Smith replied.

"Repeat after me," Robot continued. "Owha."

"Owha."

"Tasi."

"Tasi."

"Ly goo."

"Ly goo."

"Siam."

"Siam."

Robot's bright lights flashed. "Now say all the words together, Dr. Smith," he ordered.

"O what a silly goose I am," Dr. Smith said quickly.

"I'll say you are!" Major West agreed, laughing.

Penny choked back a giggle and looked at Will with surprise. "I thought you said we'd programmed all of the human humor traits out of Robot," she said.

"I must have missed a single wire connection," Will admitted. "But I kind of like him this way, don't you?"

Penny nodded. And as she watched the planet of the Blawps fade into the distance, she felt a real sense of accomplishment. She had come up with some good ideas, and grown up a lot in the process.

Penny kind of liked *herself* this way, too.